SHULAMITE WOMAN

JANEEN CHAMBERS

Originally published in 2021 in Pittsburgh, Pennsylvania
This edition published by ELF&E Productions, Dallas, Texas

Cover Art by Patigonart

Interior Formatting by JBookDesigns

Scripture taken from the New King James Version®.
Copyright © 1982 by Thomas Nelson. Used by permission. All rights reserved.

Scripture taken from the King James Version. Public Domain.

ISBN-13: 979-8711549338
ASIN: B08X69SKJF
Language: English

To my God and Heavenly Father, I am grateful for the opportunity to be a vessel through which this book was written. To my beloved children, Jalen and Savion, your encouragement and support have been astounding. To all my ladies who supported me on this journey, particularly Arielle Bateman and Orlanda Covington—thank you for your time and support!

Janeen Chambers

CHAPTER 1

His greenish-chestnut eyes, with their tints of amber, looked like jewels of some sort. His bronzed Italian skin, slightly ruddy from the summer sun, massaged my eyes. The deep sea of waves on his head became marvelous streams that traveled down the sides of his face to the square of his chin—deep black streams, flickering with moonlight slivers of gray.

He looked romantic. Distinguished.

Wow—was this man beautiful... We gazed at each other in the noonday sun as we sat on top of his car at the public theatre.

I could not wait to wake up to this man when the birds chirped. I wanted to rub my face across his lovely beard and inhale its woodsy essence, then float my fingers through those deep-sea waves that crowned him.

I wanted to be forever greeted by his smile—that fiery weapon that could melt any woman's heart. Certainly mine. It sent chills that danced up and down my spine and broke out in small bumps all over me.

I loved seeing those high cheekbones, which revealed themselves amid his echo-rich laughter. That shallow dimple that snuck out of hiding here and there...

This man looked like the authentic alpha male.

His warrior features were evident throughout his mountainous frame, which served as my wall of protection. It stood tall—chest and shoulders broad. The Predator himself would scan this man's frame and relish the challenge. I have never in my life seen someone so beautiful—almost like a Greek sculpture that had come alive. I thought this type of handsome was only to be seen on men's fitness platforms or Hollywood screens.

Often, when I left this man after a date, I didn't know whether to repent or praise God. I didn't know at times whether my excitement was aroused by adoration—or just plain ol' lust.

I was all wrapped up in the soapy beginning of love, singing **Song of Solomon** in the whispers of my mind:

> *"Let him kiss me with the kisses of his mouth, for your love is better than wine. Because of the fragrance of your good ointments, your name is ointment poured forth; therefore the virgins love you. Draw me away!"*

I definitely felt drawn away by Daniel.

I believe all women want to feel that—*drawn away*—tapped into that elusive, euphoric rapture of love. But I had to remind myself who made him. And what caught my real eyes with Daniel in the first place—my spiritual eyes.

I stopped, worshiped, and gave God the glory. I told my Heavenly Father:

> *"Father, how marvelous are Your works, for You create wonders. Thank You for reminding me of how creative and brilliant You are in the seemingly little and big things before us—like how You made Daniel."*

After I prayed this prayer, I felt balance cover me like an invisible blanket. See, every time I feel myself get weak or off-kilter, I just give it to my Father—or at least, I try to. I tell Him what I'm feeling, flat-out, in hopes that He may give me His strength in my weakness.

See, Daniel caught my eye during a mission trip to Jerusalem. My actual spiritual eye at first—not my *take me now, I'm yours* fleshly eye. Yes, even with Daniel—and I'm telling the truth.

See, I'm thirty-seven going on thirty-eight years of age. I've had plenty of fleshly-eye episodes in my youth that led me into doomsday castles—where I lost myself, my brains, and everything sane in me. I was caught up in material things and appearances. And all I received in return was deception, tears, and just... *why* and *how* situations.

I had my fair share of those—much more than I care to admit. So, I asked my Heavenly Father to open my spiritual eyes regarding my mate. I wanted to see the spirit of my mate *first* before I saw the external. And Daddy, in His kindness, had given me that ability.

During my mission trip to Jerusalem, I witnessed Daniel's electrifying heart. It gave off an energy that continually bolted insight into our thirsty minds. At that time, I just knew him as Dr. Pacini—leading his students and colleagues through Jerusalem.

Daniel was a Theological Professor and a top financial and ethics advisor. I was an event specialist. I remember when I first saw him—along with my best friend, Sheila. He was doing more talking than the actual guide. He knew the history and significance of things—places—it seemed like everything. He even knew many of the natives there. When he opened his mouth, you could see the excitement burst out of him. It was as if overwhelming rays were screaming to exit.

I remember thinking: *It's always a marvelous thing to see people in their element—in their carving—doing what God made them to do.* Their passion is contagious. A gravitational pull in its art form. A star, in a sense—lighting up a room where no shadow can stay.

I loved seeing Daniel in his element. He pulled me in.

His enthusiasm jolted every part of me. It yanked my thoughts and pulled out an inspiration that was threaded in wonder. So much substance—not for the mundane *here-today, gone-tomorrow* things—but for the real things in life: A passion for God. Family. Adventure. Love.

It was so refreshing—a cold, flowing stream in a world of dry places. It was so perfect, it almost seemed unreal. He inspired me, enticed me. It was as if his whole being revealed itself to me—the more he talked, the more he taught. I didn't even listen to the guide anymore. I think a lot of us didn't—when Daniel was present. He talked about the Great Wall, the Mount of Olives, Jesus's tomb, the tombs of the matriarchs and patriarchs... He even knew the hottest spots where we could find the best food in the land.

The landmark of the trip, however, was the baptism in the Jordan River. Something happened there that was different. A *shedding* proceeded. I had been baptized before—but being baptized in the same waters as Jesus... *wow.*

The moment became surreal.

Spiritually, I was meeting a greater epiphany. An unveiling.

I realized I was starting to see Daniel in a new way—in a new sphere—because more of his being was manifesting. I had been blind to the reason elbows nudged at my waist. I didn't notice the googly eyes, laser-focused on him—those memories came to me later.

I even recall one lady whispering under her breath, *"Boy, if I weren't married..."* But I wasn't distracted by that. I was just excited... and drawn to his spirit. Yet as the days went on, time marinated a *dissolving agent*—removing the external cloak from my eyes. The process happened gradually. It was like his *whole self* appeared—as if the Lord tapped me on my shoulder when that veil finally lifted and said: "Behold, there stands your husband."

And there he was...

God graciously gave me the ability to see the spirit first, just as I had asked. I fell in love that day with Daniel's fervent spirit. But I must say—I was floored when I saw how handsome he truly was on the outside as well. It was truly a miracle. I knew it was the Lord who had hidden all of this... This—man.

My eyes ran to his fingers—wedding ring?

No wedding ring.

Then my stomach started to flutter, and my neurons were doing backflips.

That's good—no ring—

Then not even a second later, my thoughts rushed: *Why the heck not? What's wrong with him... really?* How could he be that enormously handsome, charming, wise—and *not* be married? I guess he was waiting on me, my mind jokingly sputtered. Then another thought raced: *What is his secret?*

A burning curiosity grew in me a hundredfold. It sparked a wildfire. I started probing... and probing, subtly investigating with careful words and calm expressions. I communicated with him and his colleagues nonstop—not containing myself—allowing myself to absorb everything thrown at me, while simultaneously spilling over.

The conversations were deep, and I dove right in. So much so, that a person would've thought I belonged in their academic clique. After spending some days with them, I suppose I did. I studied their language and mannerisms. And as time went on, I gradually got to know Daniel—this intriguing stranger—along with his colleagues and his students a little better.

They were an incredible and exciting bunch—inquisitive, open, and honest. They carried a lot of substance. It was clear that Daniel was a great mentor to them. The attention and submission he received from them—and from others—was a good witness.

However, one guy seemed agitated by almost everything Daniel said. His name was Dr. Jeremy Grieves. Dr. Grieves was certainly brilliant, and a great orator like Daniel—but he had this recurring pessimism and condescension that made you want to throw up. He clearly thought he was smarter and better than everybody. His pride and arrogance jumped off him way too easily. His demeanor, however, only made Daniel stand out even more—because Daniel was so deeply rooted in humility. This strong yet gentle love... It was endearing. Personable. It was hard to believe someone so *packaged* could be so spiritually in-tune and sober-minded.

Being bathed in fascination, I had to get a bit of Daniel's backstory. I wanted to understand him. Know him. So, I asked him questions about his past—including how he was raised. I was asking the questions people wanted the answers to... The questions we were *all* wondering: *What events made this man into the man we see before us today?*

Daniel was so kind to share. And as he did, unique pieces started to gel.

Daniel was the son of a missionary pastor. In his youth, Daniel lost both of his parents. His mother gave her last breath giving birth to him, and fourteen years later, his father gave his last in a meeting in an attempt to bring the gospel to a village in the Middle East. Due to these unfortunate events, Daniel practically raised himself from the age of fourteen. The friends and family he did have, he lost on that cruel night.

Daniel stated that although he was fourteen, he made his own way due to his appearance—everyone thought he was at least seventeen or eighteen years old. He was tall and filled in for his age, and this gave him a lot of work opportunities, opening some quite unique doors – some good, and some not so good. He stated that once he removed himself a long way from the region, he started going to the library every day to have a shelter over his head during the daylight hours, but also for the free baked morning goods the receptionist laid out.

At first, Daniel said he grabbed books and looked inside just to pass the time—not really reading, but sifting through his thoughts, wondering what he would do next and where he would go. However, soon he figured that while he was there, he should at least read books he would actually like, so he started grabbing books with loud, animated covers. However, to his surprise, after some time, he began to develop a passion for reading. Daniel said that's when the scholar in him was born. He realized he loved knowledge and the act of seeking it out.

He was enamored with stories, with words, with information. So, lingering around in the library was no longer a temporary shelter; it became an exploration ground.

However, during the late-night hours, he managed to find a place to stay. These abodes were with different women who didn't care about his young age, but cared for his young body. They pushed themselves on him, using him for house fixer-uppers and lustful acts. Consequently, he lost his sexual purity and the rest of his innocence at a young age.

But, through it all, he stayed faithful to the library. So, when he was not working or with the ladies, he was at the library—there, he had peace. There, he had a sense of calmness. And there, he explored a wide range of subjects, including science, Social Science, the arts, religion, poetry, and politics. Nevertheless, he was really drawn to Theology. It grabbed onto him just as it had grabbed onto his father. It reminded him of his father. He told me his father was the most optimistic person he ever knew—even to that day. He witnessed how the words of the Holy Bible came alive through his dad. He literally saw people change through the words his father gleaned from it, so he knew what his dad practiced was something powerful, something his young mind couldn't quite grasp yet.

Later, when Daniel was in his early thirties, he discovered that hundreds of people were not only saved through his father's witness in life, but many hundreds were also saved through his father's death. He realized more than ever that even his father's death, and how it happened, had purpose in it. His witness was a beautiful vessel that God used to save thousands.

Daniel respected his father's ministry, and it was obvious. His face lit up another couple of notches when he spoke about him. Daniel also said his father practically groomed him into the reality of possible death on the mission field. So, when it happened, there was no shock or confusion, yet still, there was a very present and lingering pain. He said if it wasn't for the faithful witness of his father, he believed he would have been bitter with him, with people, with the gospel—with God. Remembering that this was his healing, just as reading and learning were—this is why the library became his sanctum. Interestingly enough, because Daniel spent so much time at the library, the chief administrative officer eventually noticed him. Enamored by his passion for knowledge, the officer offered Daniel a job as a librarian. Daniel was elated. Although hired as a librarian, he also took on a late-night security position. So often, he worked both day and night. Many nights, he slept there—falling asleep to tall tales and "ologies"—Sociology, Psychology, and more. Daniel said that from time to time, people held late meetings at the library. One night, while walking the floors, he overheard a team of people deep in debate. He couldn't help but listen; their aggravated voices demanded it.

Something lit in his chest.

The subjects, the material, the scholarship—the *art* of debate itself—intrigued him. So, he made it a point to be there every Tuesday night, walking the floor, so he could eavesdrop and analyze their discussions. He watched as the assertive professor, Earl Watts, led the group.

One night, the group were tackling the classic "isms"—Capitalism vs. Socialism. Daniel stood hidden behind the bookcases, starved—not for food, but for the content.

Then something happened.

In the middle of their conjecture, there was a snag in the progress of their argument. Daniel—still in the shadows—knew the answers and he knew just the right references and authors that could support those answers; therefore, his urge to help forced his limbs to walk out of the shadows of his hiding place and speak up.

Daniel introduced himself—then provided the answers, along with the supporting books. Through their research of his suggestions they made leaps and bounds through their argument. As a result, he was invited back. And came back, he did—every Tuesday. And every single time he returned, he added so much insight and depth that Professor Watts eventually asked him to join as their *lead researcher*. Gladly, Daniel accepted. At just eighteen years old, he joined the debate team that would soon become *undefeated*. That one opening paved the way for academic scholarships and subsequent opportunities and promotions—which helped him become Professor Daniel Pacini.

The remarkable sequence of events that shaped Daniel's life created this intelligent giant—a compassionate, humble, God-fearing giant. Just thinking too long about him gave me chills. He had a story that made me fall in love with *who* he was, more than *what* he was. I gave him a snippet of my own rocky past, too. I didn't tell him too much—at least not at first. I didn't want to frighten him. Nevertheless, our pasts seemed to bring us together in Jerusalem. We interlaced. We had a rhythm. The way we related to each other was so in sync, so in tune, it felt like we made *music* with each other's presence.

However, I felt sorry for poor Sheila—my friend who came with me on the trip. Sheila was somewhat dragged into some of our conversations, which she was not fond of. She was more interested in seeing the animals of the land and enjoyed a few of the scientific subjects we explored, but overall, she wasn't particularly interested. Still, she graciously sacrificed some of her time discerning my fancy for the golden Italian before me.

Daniel and I—and his entourage (as I called them)—talked about philosophical, spiritual, and scientific matters. We spoke about how you could see God in all of them. We even discussed simple, goofy things. I quickly discovered that Daniel and I were super nerds at heart— speaking a love language of knowledge, an ecstasy of wisdom. As the days passed during our two-week trip, I remember him staring at me more and more with eyes of wonder, especially after the baptism in the Jordan River. On the last day of the trip, he handed me this elaborate brochure.

Then he spoke.

"Opal, before we depart, you must see this and tell me what you think."

"Okay," I said, my voice soft with curiosity.

As soon as I was on the bus, I opened the brochure.

Inside was a yellow notepad, taped down with clear strips.

On the note, Daniel had drawn a single, black, lonely line.

The message was simple:

"May I contact you sometime? If you're willing, write your number here."

It was darling. Cute.

This intelligent, distinguished man sending me a grade school invitation so we could get to know each other better. How could I not?

I dove into my purse with lightning speed.

Sheila gave me the "calm-down" eyes as she watched me shuffle and fumble, searching for at least one pen or writing utensil. My behavior was suddenly erratic. I had never reacted in such an energized way before. Sure, when a guy asked for my number, I'd get excited or maybe a little anxious—especially if I liked him. But *this*? This was different. This feeling was new territory. I do believe it was also a symptom of my five-year span of singleness that contributed to me falling for this diamond-in-the-rough of a man.

But I had to keep my composure and follow the cue in Sheila's eyes to take a breather. I might scare off this intellectual king who had finally arrived to knock me off my feet. I finally found the pen—buried in my large, disorganized purse, which was stuffed with all the promotional ads I'd picked up on the trip. I took a deep breath and calmed my nerves by counting backwards from twenty. Once I regained my composure, I wrote in my best cursive:

Please email me first. I love getting to know you, but I believe this is the best way.

This response let him know I was interested—but also that he'd need to do some chasing if he wanted my phone number.

Yeah... I know.

My stance was an oxymoron in itself.

I didn't want to immediately give him my number—although every part of me was screaming, *Girl—you crazy—you better give him your number.* Underneath all of the loud excitement was a calm call for self-control. I wanted to do things differently even in the midst of my crush. I *knew* he had ladies storming down his door. I wanted to add a little mystery. And looking back—honestly—I'm glad I did.

As we entered the bus on our way home, I handed him the brochure he'd given me earlier—now with my response taped inside. Then I looked at him with intentionally bright eyes.

"Professor, that was pretty informative. Thanks for sharing," I said with a delicate smile—not too overbearing, not too short.

He smiled back—greatly. So much so, I couldn't help but blush through my brown skin. I could feel my cheekbones rising—and I couldn't stop them—so I swiftly turned to my seat, trying to hide the face that exposed it all. Eventually, Sheila and I arrived at our respective homes. And then—excitedly—the next day, I received an email from Daniel.

From there—it was on.

We messaged each other for at least a good week. He seemed to love the chase. I suppose it was because he usually didn't have to pursue. I'm sure he had numbers aggressively flying at him from all four corners of the earth. So, I assumed he found it refreshing to have to chase the feline. One of the craziest things, though? We were practically neighbors—almost. He lived and taught in Virginia. I lived in North Carolina. It was wild that we met so far away in Jerusalem, only to find out we resided relatively close to each other back home.

We emailed frequently—outside of our work schedules, and occasionally during them too. I'm pretty sure we were checking our emails the way most people check their texts. By the end of the week, he implored me to give him my phone number. And I did—because I was beat up from email exhaustion, too.

As the last strokes of my fingers tapped the buttons to my number, I realized: I had taken the power out of my hands and placed it into his.

Now *I* was the one waiting.

And wait... I did.

It was almost like he was trying to get me back for having him wait for my number—with a lot of nail biting and feet tapping, I waited. An entire day went by. Anxiety was certainly making her bed as I constantly checked my phone.

Then…Then… Daniel called. Heyyyyy….

Finally, it was like a blanket, a fireplace, and hot cocoa for my overworked nerves. Yeah, the initial call was calming, but his voice contributed. It was just as I remembered: deep and melting. I was lost in it, and especially the content that flowed from it. The conversation was amazing, and that phone call lasted through the night and into the wee hours of the morning. I was so in love, captivated by the fact that I could talk into another human being and he could talk back into me, like we'd known each other for years, when we'd really only known each other for weeks. I believe when we hung up that night, we both realized that this was real—and deep. We felt something more, and that more grabbed onto our souls and bared down. At least I felt that.

Now fast-forward, a little over one year later—we were an engaged couple, a unique couple at that. See, Daniel is half Italian and half Israeli. He states that the half-Israeli side is tied to his Hebrew roots. Now, I, Opal Cleverson, am of African American descent. I am a darker-skinned, brown woman. I consider myself a slender curvy. I have light, hazel-brown eyes, which set off a clear contrast against my dark skin. These light eyes always evoke the question—Are they yours? Which I have to respond with exhaustion—yes. I guess I am a little taller than the average height woman. I wear my natural curls, without the use of chemicals or extensions. I either wear my hair in long individual twists, a poufy French roll, or in a massive curly Diana Ross draping fro—Daniel called it that anyway, which he loved. I suppose I'm an okay-looking lady. Daniel thinks I am beautiful, and that is all that matters.

Sometimes Daniel looked at me with amazement, as if I were some exotic animal in the zoo, and it seemed he couldn't get enough of my hair. He was always touching it, patting it, running his fingers through it, although his fingers would get caught sometimes through my web of tight curls—Hee, hee. Sometimes he acted like it was a pillow of some sort when we talked to each other well into the night in his truck on summer nights. He continuously grazed his vein-popping, strong hands over my face and kissed my cheeks and told me how he adored me. He spoke into my uniqueness, saying I was his unique beauty, his Shulamite woman. I loved this part of him almost the most, second to his love for our Heavenly Father. Our heart beats drummed the same tune. We both loved the Lord, wanted to serve the Lord with our lives, and we wanted to serve and lavishly love each other through Him.

The closer Daniel and I became, the more I needed to spend time with my Heavenly Father. I felt at times that maybe I was idolizing this man. I felt twinges of myself gravitating towards that. I couldn't help but think about him all the time and speak about him all the time. He seemed to be, so... perfect. The man of every woman's dream, the actual real, fledged-out, handsome, twenty-first-century knight coming to save me in his fitted, open-collared shirt. I mean, I couldn't help but think, *"Am I dreaming? Is this really happening to me? Ok, ok, I'm about to wake up any minute now...but no...I am awake—oh goodie."* I absolutely adored him; that is why my constant prayer during this time was to keep Daniel in his proper place and not forget The Great Beauty who made him, my First Love.

But throughout all this beautiful aura of awe, there stood a thorn. Surprise-surprise! What relationship does not have one.

This thorn—women—and more women.

These females were constantly, I mean constantly, throwing themselves over him. It was as if he were some international movie star at times. They acted like they needed to see him, feel him—which really pumped fire up my chimney. At times, it seemed Daniel loved the attention. However, because it was becoming so loud and bold—I didn't know what to do. I seemed to be in this process of adoring him and then on the other hand being this overprotective, paranoid mess, wondering if a woman prettier than me or more godly than me would pull him away.

I mean, these ladies did not care, unfortunately, either out of the church or in the church. The desperate disposition of the women for their Adam manifested itself when Daniel came around. It's like I could feel the very heat radiating off these ladies' bodies so hotly that sometimes I just wanted to go dump some holy water on them to see if they'd melt.

I couldn't believe how loud these women were sometimes, especially when I was standing right next to him. I could quickly smell the aroma of a fake as well—no matter how innocent she made herself out to be. A woman would not even have to say a word, and I felt her heated Potiphar's wife intentions, and it seemed the heat rose even higher when he spoke. Well, I understand...that is how I fell in love with him.

Funny thing... as a theological professor, he seemed to always have a packed house. People, primarily women, lined up to opt into his courses. So, I thought, *what am I to do about this? I did not know...*

Nevertheless, I did receive a revelation about the situation. Through Daniel, I discovered that beauty, charm, and skill could be, in and of themselves, a person's plight. The person who had all these worldly gifts was always faced with a greater seduction of self-glory and/or alluring temptations, and the one loving him or her was always faced with a heightened sense of these realities feasibly taking their love away.

Because Daniel and I were engaged to be married in a month, and I was having all these episodes with all these crazy women, fear climbed into my lungs and seized them. My past—with knuckle-headed men, especially one—aided in this, they planted an insecurity in me that fear took advantage of. And although I knew I was crazy about Daniel, the fear was very real and erratic, and it birthed something with Daniel that was not there before: doubt.

It seemed this doubt alongside fear continued to pile on top of me like a layered cake, and the war in my head was beginning to be constant and thunderous. A battleground that measured Daniel's goodness vs rejection, again.

CHAPTER 2

I knew I had to talk to my sisters to get some clarity. My circle of sisters is a solid group of four: Sheila, Purple, Angel, and Samantha. They're my spiritual clique.

Purple is the oldest—the spiritual mother of the group. She's a lighter-complected African American woman, so fair-skinned she could pass for Caucasian if it weren't for her full lips and naturally afro-textured hair. Purple has very distinct features: long, golden eyelashes and thick, golden brows that she keeps flawlessly arched. Faint golden freckles are sprayed symmetrically across her cheekbones. She's slightly obese, very heavy-chested, with a round pooch in her belly—yet she has skinny legs.

Purple is a preacher's wife, an organic mother by nature—even though she has no children. It's a bit ironic, considering she came from a big family of twelve: seven sisters and five brothers. As the eldest, she served as the second mother in the household, and that title—whether spiritual or biological—followed her everywhere she went.

Then there is Sheila, who came with me to Jerusalem. Sheila is one of my oldest and dearest friends. She is half Korean and half African American. She has light-tanned skin, and a mystique radiates from her stellar, slanted eyes. Her unique fusion of genes makes her hair absolutely fabulous—jet black and thick—definitely commercial-worthy. She keeps it organic, styled in a chin-length bob. Sheila's features are slender and sharp. She is model-thin and gracefully tall—a mirror of elegance and gentleness.

By trade, Sheila is a veterinarian. I remember, even when we were kids, she loved animals. Sheila's house was like a miniature, eclectic farm. She had two rabbits, three dogs, cats, fish, a hamster, chickens, and even a pig we called Sammy, whom she constantly clothed with a red or blue handkerchief. When an animal became sick or passed—whether it was her pet or not—she was like the saddest person I'd ever met.

Then there is Angel. Angel was the baby of our circle—the spiritual and emotional mentee we all felt compelled to take under our wings. She was raised in the Bronx, New York. She often said she wasn't just from the melting pot, she *was* the melting pot—a mixture of the browns.

Her mother is half Brazilian and half African, and her father is Mexican, so her skin is wonderful—butter-brown and tanned, with an extra glow. She has big, light-brown puppy eyes and round curls that are big and soft. Her teeth aren't necessarily all straight, but they have character in their lack of uniformity—which adds even more charm to her amazing smile.

She has a muscular, curvaceous build like Serena Williams—a testament to her being an incredibly talented physical trainer. Although her urban, hood vernacular sometimes deceives people into thinking she isn't highly educated, at just twenty-seven, she holds degrees in Kinesiology, Human Anatomy, and Nutrition Science.

Then there is Samantha. Samantha has a very sensual look—like a mermaid who received her legs and became trapped in the fifties. She has that classic, curvy, old-Hollywood movie star aura. Samantha is Caucasian, with fiery red hair, which she keeps slicked back in a perfectly neat ponytail bun—or leaves loose in voluminous, deep-wave tresses. She has moon-pale skin and ocean-blue eyes. She is marvelous.

Samantha is a judge by profession—sharp and just in her practice. She isn't quite liberal or conservative—she wears her objective hat well. She would say she's a woman of truth. And indeed, that she is. She's one of those people who always seem two or three steps ahead of you. The years of debate and competition her parents enrolled her in from early childhood clearly shaped her persona.

Samantha and Purple are my mentors. Samantha walked with me through my long, single journey of five years. As beautiful as she is, she's been single for eleven. She helped me realize the growth that needed to take place within me before I would be ready for the true man I desired—and the one God had for me. Meeting Samantha, it's clear that she is wise, fierce, and a little stubborn—traits that, I believe, stem from a bitter root. Still, she is fair. And ninety percent of the time... she's right. So, a man must be quite a man to come alongside her. Few men like that are made anymore. It seems they either meet her and become intimidated by her force—or grow combative in response to their own pride.

Angel spoke with a slight roll of her eyes, responding to my plight with these women and my growing doubt about Daniel.

"I'm saying, Miss O, I know we're supposed to be all classy... right and everything, but I'm just gonna say it—Daniel is fine as h-e-double hockey sticks. I wouldn't let that go."

"What..." the ladies all said in unison.

"Seriously, Angel," Sheila spouted.

"I didn't say it—what y'all trippin' about? I literally spelled it out," Angel shot back.

"Honey, there is nothing fine about no hell," Purple stressed, her eyes cutting into mine.

Giggles rose from the group.

"Angel, the question is, could she handle all of what comes with Daniel—not Daniel himself?" Purple asked.

"Somebody else will—besides, the wedding is a month away," Angel said, pursing her lips.

Sheila butted in. "We're not talking about a breakup—are we? It's not that bad. You know Daniel's heart."

"I think I do... but as perfect as Daniel is—no one is really that perfect except Jesus. And... Daniel had his womanizing days..." I said.

"Daniel had womanizing days?" Sheila asked.

"That's it then," Samantha butted in.

"What?"

"Your fight. Because I was wondering too, like—this guy is too perfect." From Samantha's tone, it was clear she'd been waiting all along for something to come up about Daniel.

"I wouldn't care about any lady if I'm bringing Daniel home every day," Angel interrupted.

"Young lady, your hormones are blocking your frontal cortex right now," Purple said, pursing her lips.

"Mrs. Purple, I know all about your frontal cortex—this is rational, not just emotional."

Angel glanced around the table.

"I'm sorry, ladies—but y'all acting like Mr. Daniel is not fine. Come on now, be real. I ain't never seen anyone that looks like Mr. Daniel. And I work in the physical fitness world—and he loves Jesus! It is very rational to think: *Hey, this is my gift from God—I'm snatching him up. Quick!*"

Sheila and I chuckled, but Purple shook her head.

"She knows that. We know he's attractive and all, Hun—but that's not everything. That in and of itself seems to be the challenge for Opal—because of all it's bringing with all the women, and how it's making her feel all the time—not some of the time. Now, you know I'm the first one to say feelings are fleeting—but they do tell you something, either about yourself, or about someone around you who might be imparting that onto you.

You've got to figure out if it's you or the other who's consistently making those *whatever* feelings arrive.

Sheila butted in, munching on the last of her salad.

"I don't know, O—maybe he *is* doing something. I'm not saying he's cheating, necessarily. But maybe he's giving off some type of intentional vibe that gives these ladies the green light to do what they're doing. I'm just saying—it's not like he's some rock star."

"I beg to differ," said Purple.

"Well, he *is* a rock star in a way," I cut in. "He's a best-selling author, he's on TV debating or advising practically every week, and he keeps a packed class..."

"Yeah—the lady from that one show called him *the Hot Prophet*," Purple blurted.

Samantha cut in, one brow raised.

"Did you tell them about *Red Rain*?"

"Red Rain—*Whaaat?*" Angel blinked in confusion.

"Rain what?" Purple echoed.

Then Purple glanced at my twisted lip—and the meaning of the conversation dawned on her.

"Oh... you're talking about the red pantie that fell out of the book?" she exclaimed.

"Well, Angel and Sheila don't know," I said, thinking about that pantie.

I shook my head and took a long sip of tea.

Then Sheila leaned forward, diving her head into the nucleus of our circle.

"Red panties falling out of whose book—Daniel's?"

"Yep," I said, taking another swallow.

Angel and Sheila locked eyes in stunned silence—then quickly snapped their heads back to me, eager for more.

"Why—what happened?" Angel asked.

"Well, I was coming to see Daniel for lunch because we hadn't seen each other for a couple of days. It was electrifying, as always. After he dismissed the class he came and picked me up. We kissed...." I said, smiling through my teeth.

"Ooooh—when y'all start kissing?" Angel asked, wide-eyed.

"After he proposed," Sheila jumped in.

"I thought y'all were waiting for marriage—keeping y'all self pure," Angel said.

"We are—we haven't had sex... yet. And we don't plan to until marriage," I replied.

"We just embrace and kiss. We decided to kiss after the proposal. Well, we didn't originally plan to—it's just that after I said yes, he rose from his knee and started kissing me. It was perfect. So, we decided to just kiss and embrace until we become one."

"Umm... you better than me, Ms. Opal," Angel said.

"Why is that?" I asked.

"I would've been gave him some—or gave me some—however you'd like to put it. I'm sorry," Angel said with a chuckle.

"Trifling," Samantha belted.

All the ladies looked at Angel.

"Ms. Sam, don't start—I'm just keeping it authentic."

Angel felt the eyes of the ladies quietly scolding her.

"What—I'm sorry, ladies. Pray for me. I ain't there yet. Y'all know I keeps it real—that's how we grow, right ladies? By first being real with ourselves."

She said it in a way to try to ease back the ladies. It worked to some degree, though a few of them still shook their heads. I spoke.

"Being celibate is hard. Very hard. Especially because we're so attracted to each other. But God is who we look at first, instead of ourselves—that's what being a living sacrifice is all about. In this case, for Daniel and me, it means throwing our desires for each other on the altar until the right time. But honey... when the time comes, it's going to be explosive. It'll be just us—discovering each other for the first time, intimately. No bars. He'll be all mine, and I'll be all his. Actually, it sounds exciting and fun to me—like an awaited scavenger hunt into ecstasy. A Christmas gift I can't open until Christmas day!"

"God's ways are always the best!" Sheila said, shaking her shoulders in a delightful shrug.

"All stuff, Ms. Opal—y'all gon' have that next-level sacred sex. The type Sheila and her man be having, huh…" Angel said in a playful whisper.

"Whaaat... y'all ain't supposed to share stuff like that. That's for you and your husband only," Purple chimed in.

"See, that's why I don't tell you stuff, Angel," Sheila responded.

The ladies started laughing.

"I feel you, Ms. O—but Mr. Daniel... Daniel... *whew*, you got all that—I know I couldn't do it!" Angel stated. Purple butted in.

"Angel, Hun, the key is to keep your eyes on Jesus—focused on Him. Because yes, in ourselves, honey... we just can't do it. There is *nothing* strong in this thing called flesh we wear every day."

Purple pinched her own arm—then Angel's. Then she continued:

"The moment we focus too much on our own desires, we become consumed by them. And *that* is dangerous, because this very thing—this overconsumption of ourselves—can dim us from what is truly right."

Purple lifted her arm up. And continued.

"That's why, to become better—to *be* better—we must look beyond ourselves. That's why I said focus on Jesus. Because *Him* being Light will remove every dark, lost, and struggling place in us." But it takes time to understand this. We are being sanctified daily. And all that means is we are being renewed in our minds every day by walking more out of our impulses—the flesh—and more and more into the Spirit of God."

Grunts of agreement came out from the ladies.

Purple laid her hand on Angels, then continued:

"But I understand your fight—the pastor and I came *quite* close, so it's not easy. Amen, ladies?"

All the ladies said together, "AMEN!"

"Not fun. The waiting period is *real*—but it was worth it," Sheila said in a way that tattled secrets behind her words.

"That's what I'm saying. I love Jesus—y'all know that—but sometimes it feels like we can't have fun," Angel snickered.

Sheila burst in.

"Girl, you know that's a lie—that's the total opposite. God *made* fun. He created sex in the first place—matter of fact, He engineered our bodies to experience. We could've been mating with no feeling, or eating *clay.*

I'm thankful He created sex... *girl...* I'm so thankful. And I'm thankful for my *palate...* I can eat ice cream."

"Chocolate," Samantha butted in.

"Yes, Chile! And I can taste that southern-baked mac and cheese with all the cheeses and crusts on top," said Purple.

"Potato salad and peach cobbler," Samantha added.

"What is this, Thanksgiving?" I butted in.

Sheila responded. "No, we became hungry real quick. See, Angel—look where all that food restriction has gotten us. How did sex turn into food in 0.1 seconds?"

We all chuckled.

"*You're* the one who brought both of them up," stated Angel.

Shrugs and confused nods circled the group of ladies, then greater laughter arose.

"Oh yeah," Sheila said, "That's why I brought up food. Taste and sex tell us He wants us to enjoy—experience. The parameters are *for our sake* so we can also have *future* joy. Self-control can tap us into that—not things controlling *us*."

"Right, right, right... speak that, Sheila," I chimed in.

Samantha's silky voice intervened.

"It's the *hastiness* in life that waters things down, it skips crucial steps... or omits much-needed things. Waiting, darling, gives you substance—value—nothing cheap.

And the wait is used to adopt a spirit of self-control as Sheila alluded to—to establish rulership in us—*not* to make slaves out of us, which unchecked impulses can do."

Angel stormed in.

"I'm saying... don't y'all ever want to do something wild? *Crazy*?!"

"*Chile*. Been there, done that," Purple said.

"I did wild and crazy—and learned from it!" she added.

"Mrs. Purple, I can't see *you* doing anything wild and crazy," Angel said, rolling her eyes.

"Hun—I was young *once*. That ends that argument," Purple stated.

Laughter pressed.

"Who says you have to let go of wild and crazy...it depends on the context. My hubby and I can get a little wild and crazy," Sheila added.

"We know!" we all concerted together—then laughed.

"*TMI, Chile... TMI*," Purple chimed.

Samantha intervened: "The point is, we are created to have fun—to be free—to enjoy. But it comes with responsibility. So the parameters we're talking about, the ones that are set forth, are there to protect us. *Every word of God is sculpted to protect.* To protect... is to love."

"Okay, Mrs. Deep—always taking us into the middle of the Pacific Ocean somewhere," Angel stated.

We all laughed, but as always, we respected Samantha's words. So, we started snapping our fingers—even though Angel rolled her eyes while doing it. She had to give Samantha, Purple, and Sheila their props—even if she didn't like their meddling words.

Snapping our fingers was something we all did when someone spoke something of real substance. Samantha and Purple were good for evoking those moments. We actually copied that finger-snapping tradition from an audience at a poetry jam we saw together one night.

"I get it. I just don't see how *y'all* do it though," Angel rebutted.

"Well, what do you mean by *y'all*? Mrs. Purple and I are married—we get it all the time. Well... *I* think. I don't know about Mrs. Purple, but I know I do."

"Chile, you better leave me alone," Purple responded.

Continued laughter left our mouths and pressed into the air.

"Probably not as much as *you*, Mrs. Sheila Wayans," Purple added, "but we have our times... Not that I should be sharing that with *you* ladies," she said with a friendly roll of her eyes.

Then she latched back onto the topic. "But we had our season of celibacy too."

"Do you trust Him?" Samantha interrupted.

"Trust who?" Angel replied. Samantha gave Angel that stare—the one that whips people back on track in her courtroom. Angel instantly knew what was translating from Samantha's mouth.

"God—of course!" Angel said with sincerity.

"Then trust Him with your temple too—He got you, sweetie," Purple interjected.

Then, after Purple's words left the air, Samantha cut in. "Okay, back to the subject—Opal, you were talking about meeting Daniel in his class."

It dawned on the ladies that they had gotten off a tantalizing topic. Angel and Sheila shook their heads as if in a trance coming back to reality, and Purple leaned back slightly.

"Oh yeah—and Opal, get them to the goodies. Don't drag out the story; you always do that," stated Purple.

"Seriously?" I responded.

"I'm sorry, you *do* do that," Samantha agreed.

"I keep encouraging her to write a book," Angel added.

Giggles swirled.

I received the message with a side movement of my jaw and a little nod.

"Oh, ladies—it's like that?"

"Aww, don't be upset, O, you know we love you," Sheila said, rubbing my back.

I knew she was trying to smooth out any small offense they may have created.

"Anyway…You ladies want to hear? Yes or no?" I asked.

"Okay, just go ahead," Purple said.

All the ladies either chuckled or giggled.

I continued. "So, after we talked for some time, I noticed an interesting book on his desk—it looked like it was on naturalism versus the supernatural. But when I picked it up, a note fell out… along with some red panties."

"*Whaaaaat?*" Angel and Sheila said simultaneously.

"I grabbed the note and the panties quickly—which I *cannot* believe I did. I guess my anger drained my common sense or something. I held them both up for Daniel to see and said,

'What is this?'" He stuttered and then said—*(I imitated a deep voice the best way I could)*:

"'I don't even know—I promise I didn't know those were in there—I'm sorry. I don't know what to say.'"

"His unbelievable words danced on every nerve I had. I felt lava rising from my chest to my head.

Then I responded:

'Well, let's see then. Let's read the note.'"

Then he says, "'Well, Opal… you can do that, but I don't believe it's something that would be good…being what fell out.'"

"I gave him a flaming Superman stare that could've lasered right through him and burnt that letter into dust. I drove my red eyes quickly over the cursive letters on the paper. In the letter, this woman called herself *Red Rain*—why, I do not know. She certainly sounded how I felt at that moment."

"What in the world? *Red Rain*— what is she, on her period?" Purple interrupted.

"*Mrs. Purple, that's nasty,*" I stated.

"Well, what are we *supposed* to think?" Purple countered.

Angel began chuckling—laughing so hard she started coughing up some of her smoothie.

Then Angel's reaction spurred giggles between us that pressed into the atmosphere.

"Red Rain… like *why*?" Sheila said.

"Because she be making red panties rain out of dudes' books!" Angel said with a deep-echo laugh.

Small laughter chased hers.

"You all, stop. I am seriously in a dilemma," I pressed.

The laughter dwindled as they witnessed my firm expression.

"Seriously, Opal—she sounds like a *psycho*," Samantha spouted.

"Yep, sure does to me," added Angel.

"Are you ladies going to allow me to finish telling you the story?"

Nods, waves of the hands, and commencing gestures gave me the moment I needed to proceed.

"Ladies, this woman was talking about how she was *so in love* with Daniel—and that she thought their reunion would be both natural *and* supernatural. She then went on to explain all her fantasies of him and her while they were in class. It was just… *yuck*. It made me so angry."

"What did Daniel say?" Sheila asked.

"*He stated, 'I will report this to the dean. I have received notes like this over the years, but never this sexually explicit. Opal, trust me—this is some lady's issue, nothing more.'*"

"His words, ladies, were *formless* against my rage. I asked him, 'Daniel, why did she give you the note and the panties in the *same way* you communicate with *me* in secret? How did she know how to reach you like that—through a *book*!?'"

"Because, ladies, since day one, Daniel and I have always communicated this way—through meetings or classes, via brochures, books, and/or material with little notes inside—which *he* initiates."

"His response? He shrugged his shoulders, and his face turned a little pink. I *knew* something was wrong from his reaction. I threw the note and the panty—which, oddly enough, smelled like *peppermint*—down on his desk. Why I had the panty in my hand so long...I don't know. I grabbed the antibacterial solution from his desk, which sat beside a picture of *me*, squirted it on my hands, and stormed out of his office."

Shaking heads and thinking expressions consumed the ladies.

Then Angel broke the brief silence.

"You made sure you squirted that antibacterial solution on your hands though."

Giggles pressed.

"I hope you *washed* your hands after that too," Sheila added.

"Lady, you *know* I did," I responded.

"Well, Opal—what are you thinking?" Purple asked, calming the ladies with her tone.

"Well...based on the letter, there was *some* indication—through her language—that they had a recent past. Her phrasing clearly communicated she was anticipating *more*. It's just— she knew to send this message the way Daniel usually initiates things with *me*, in secret."

"Yeah, that does sound shady," Angel interrupted.

"Did you ask him if *he* initiated it? Maybe he did communicate with others like that in the *past*, Opal. The *past*," said Purple.

"No, I just stormed out."

Samantha butted in.

"Well, I think you should gather a little more evidence and totally hear from him before you come to any serious conclusions— especially about doubting the whole relationship. And like Angel stated earlier...the wedding is in a month."

CHAPTER 3

I looked around after coming down off my rage high and saw the mess it caused: a tipped over table, large, staring eyes, wine splattered on clothes, still, shocked expressions, and shakings' of the heads that shouted disappointment.

At that moment, I felt a boulder of shame crash into my chest, and tears flowed down my cheeks like a rockless stream. I quickly scanned the room again—then locked eyes with Daniel's flushed red face and then the embarrassment on him jumped onto me. It possessed me, it forced my body to snap back to the exit and run—run completely away.

As my feet picked up speed, I heard Daniel's voice calling my name. It echoed through the walls of the event. I found myself outside and then that strong hand I know so well stopped me. I was a slave to his strength as he pulled me toward him. He spiraled me into his arms and gave me a frustrated stare.

"Opal, why aren't you getting it?!"

Then he stopped, grabbed my face, and kissed me with a passion that dissolved almost every facet of stubborn will in me. Slowly, he moved his pressed lips away from mine and stared into my eyes for a long couple of seconds.

"Under God, Opal... my heart beats only for you," he growled, and then pressed his lips against mine again. My spirit was being drawn back to him—almost. But then...

I opened my eyes. Bright red caught my peripheral. I looked. And there she was—*again.*

That Red Rain woman. The one who'd agitated the whole night. She swirled her thin hips in that red dress, and her red, red scarf fluttered in the wind as she walked away. But then—she turned, and unapologetically blew Daniel a kiss.

Anger. Embarrassment. Jealousy. Fear.

It rose again, that perfect storm that caused me to unload in the event had just begun to subside. But sadly, Red Rain's action made me grip instead of let go. Then suddenly, I was reminded of all the ladies, my constant torment of jealousy with them, and what a monster it made of me in that place. I closed my eyes, and it seemed like the cold rain drops that soaked through my dress became warm, probably from the heat radiating off my body. I would not be surprised if literal steam was lifting off me. My emotions were everywhere, stirring another chemical reaction to another explosion. But oddly enough, within the torment of my emotions a single answer came to me that brought a moment of relief, an answer that would kill all of this, the only answer I thought was best. I opened my eyes and stared into his jewels—knowing it might be the last time I would see them. Then I opened my mouth:

"I'm sorry, Daniel... I can't do this anymore."

"What do you mean—what are you saying?" Daniel said with a deep baritone I hadn't heard before, so deep, it rattled my insides.

I yanked my hand out of his strong grip and ran down the street to my car. I didn't look back. I picked up speed like a track star in heels, then dashed into my vehicle. I started the engine even though I heard him screaming my name.

Then, I looked through my dripping window and I saw Daniel dashing towards the car soaked in distress—*that man caught up with me fast,* I thought. Then, snapping back to my hurt, I turned my head towards the road and peeled off. I drove—away—away from all the drama, the vehement jealousy, the revealing of breasts against the interviewer's glass, the ruby lipstick on his collar, the secret notes, and the wanton eyes. But I also drove away from my best friend, my companion, and the man I can talk with when the sun goes down and when it rises back up. The man I can make love to without one physical touch or sexual thought. The man whose company entertains me in a way no other has ever done.

I drove and drove and drove. I didn't head home, I just drove around, a complete, hot, emotional mess. Finally, after hours of pathetic dread, I decided to park, and when I finally did, another level of pain, grief, and embarrassment took over me. It hovered over me and then entered every part of my body causing it to ache. Just thinking about not seeing Daniel again hurt me so, it left my body groaning.

Loud knuckles slammed on my window. I looked up with tear-swollen eyes and saw Purple. She was clothed in a purple satin head wrap and an ankle-length white robe. She was looking at me with eyes that stated she was tortured with concern. I looked a couple of feet away from her and realized I was parked outside her house and didn't even know it. My subconscious had taken over and driven me straight to a place I felt the safest.

Purple's muffled screaming of my name penetrated my car door and shook me into full consciousness. She told me to open the door. I did, and my body slumped out. She immediately grabbed my limbs and hollered for her husband to help me. Purple tried to lift my head and look through the doors to my soul, but I would not hold my head up. I felt completely defeated. I felt horrible, weak, and so riddled in melancholy I felt sick.

Pastor Chris came out with sort of a limp, trying his best to come down those cobblestone steps swiftly. He'd had knee surgery a couple of months ago. Seeing this, I told Purple, with what little breath I felt I had, that I couldn't have Pastor trying to lift me up—I could walk. So, I stood completely up from my dramatic, moping position and immediately felt pain run up my spine. I started to walk up the colorful cobblestone steps. Pastor was trying to balance me, but I thought I better balance him as he sort of leaned into me up the steps.

I didn't know why Purple called him.

When we reached the porch, Purple opened the screen door for me to enter into her haven. I did and immediately entered into citrus and floral scents. I sat down on one of her plastic-seated, light oak chairs.

"Now child what has happened to you?" Pastor Chris asked.

I looked at him, full of despair. My thoughts did not want to move into his direction and my lips did not want to function. I just wanted to be left alone, but simultaneously, I didn't. I wanted Purple and not another man at this time, although it was Pastor Chris, who I respected greatly. I just needed Purple's nurturing spirit. *That's why I was led here* I thought.

"I'm sorry, Pastor Chris, I don't want to disrespect you, but can I talk to Mrs. Purple?"

Pastor Chris looked at Purple with compassionate eyes and mushed lips, then he turned his head toward me and nodded.

"Of course, you go right ahead then. I hope you feel better."

Pastor Chris wobbled into the other room. Then Purple dived deeper into my sphere, and I dove into her bosom. With childish cries, I dove—because I lost my favorite toy, my best friend, my love. Purple put her hand on my chin and lifted it with her thumb and pointer finger to finally gaze into my open but straining doors.

"What has knocked your spirit so much that you can hardly use your breath and your limbs?"

Before I could muster up a word, which was hard, she saw the answer in my eyes—as if my pupils formulated a sudden message of the culprit, which only she could see. In a short, deep response, she spoke. "Daniel."

Purple continued, "Opal, baby, what happened?"

I couldn't muster the strength to speak, but just cried. *That question*—it aroused the next wave of outcry within me. I wailed.

"It's alright. You don't have to say anything right now—just let it out," Purple said as her eyes frowned. She started to rock me as I cried. She allowed me to vent and release through wailings, but no words. She just held me as I sunk deeper into her bosom—and that is why I needed… *her.*

CHAPTER 4

*M*y eyelids dragged up and down, trying to lift the invisible weights that seemed to hold them down. My eyes scanned. I found myself tucked into thick cotton sheets. Artfully arranged, decorated quotes and unique flower pictures adorned the walls. I knew where I was. I smelled bacon in the air, peppers, cinnamon—*umm, breakfast*. It caused a stir in my belly. My neglected belly was shaking its fist at me, revolting from lack of nourishment. So, I moved to go get some food.

I pulled back the white sheets and immediately felt chilled from the air-conditioned room. But before I raised up, I realized I needed a second—a second to collect my thoughts, to make sense of the last looney days which were flying through my head like lightning. My mind rewound: the red, the anger, her beauty, the confusion, the deception, the doubt—*sorrow*. I dived deeper into my thoughts, and the pressure increased. Then suddenly, the pressure stalled—halted by a soft, cool wind from an opening door and then... white fluffy slippers.

I looked up slowly, knowing that frame and smell—Purple.

Purple looked tortured in her face, but her Sunday best stated she was quite the opposite: bright and happy. She was dressed in a fuchsia pink dress with a sparkling crystal neckline, which matched her crystal-studded earrings.

"How are you, love?"

"I guess I'm fine," I said swiftly.

"Umm?" Purple questioned with just a grunt.

I lifted my head further, and my eyes inadvertently landed centered into her truth pullers. The truth flowed.

"No... I'm not totally fine. But I guess I feel a smidgen better."

Purple smirked, then walked to my side and nudged me to get up.

"Come, have some breakfast before church."

"Well, Purple, I don't know if I am going to make it..." I said, while heightening my exhaustion.

Purple read it immediately and dropped her head, cutting off my words with a stern expression. Being scolded by her eyes, I gave in. I had no strength to resist. I gave it all away in cries.

"Ok, ok—but I have no change of clothes."

"That's already taken care of." I looked at Purple with soft curiosity.

"Sheila already went to your house and gathered up some clothes for you," she said.

"Sheila? Purple, who all knows that I'm here?" I asked, tilting my head toward her. "It was not my fault, Opal. Daniel was so concerned about you that he called everybody and their mamma telling them how you two fell out the other night—not leaving any details, but just saying you left all distraught. He even called me looking for you, but I didn't pick up, so I wouldn't be forced to lie. But the man has called me over seven times."

I shook my head.

"Where is Sheila now?" I asked.

"In the kitchen. With the rest of the ladies."

"The rest of the ladies? Seriously, Purple?" I murmured.

"Daniel alerted them to the situation, Opal, not I. I simply told them you were okay when they called looking for you. I told them you were safe and with me, so they weren't swelling up with worry. Because everyone—including Daniel—showed up at your house, and when you weren't there, they decided to come over here.

"But yes, I did tell Sheila to get some clothes for you so you could make it to church today—knowing she's the only one with an extra key to your home. You've been in that room for a couple of days, you know."

Wow, I thought to myself. A couple of days.

"By the way, Daniel knows you're okay—we told him. He just doesn't know that you're with me. Nevertheless, your sisters are here, and they're here to be supportive and make sure you're alright."

"Okay…" I stated begrudgingly.

Purple won her argument.

I knew I had to prepare. Prepare my mind for all the questions and concerns the ladies were about to dash at me. It's not like I wouldn't tell them eventually—it's just that I didn't know if I was ready for them at that moment.

I walked into Purple's lilac-painted bathroom across the hall from me and shut the door. I looked around briefly, but then locked my eyes onto the grand Sleeping Beauty mirror on my left. The gold frame caught my eye from the rising sun bouncing off it through the window. It was beautiful. But my admiration quickly withered when I saw my reflection.

Oh, my goodness. I looked like I had just come off the corner strung out on something. I guess in a sense, I was. The Daniel drug—and withdrawal was killing me. My hair looked smashed, like jet-black cotton candy. I had a crater of crust in both corners of my eyes and one exiting my nostril. Those big craters told the story of the wet lava that had relentlessly poured out not too long ago. My artificial lashes, which I rarely wear, were crooked and barely holding on, waiting for a rescue team. My skin? Desert dry—I'm sure from all the liquid salt smeared on it. My eyelids were still swollen, and the whites of my eyes held a tint of pink.

I took a moment of uninterrupted stillness in my head and just looked at myself. Then a thought surfaced: *Opal, wash your face and anoint your body with oil. It's a new day.* As I looked down, I saw a preparation. On Purple's marble sink were clean, white folded towels, a white washcloth, and my Shea Butter and Shea Butter soap, which I knew Sheila had grabbed for me. They sat atop the cloths like special toppings. Next to them was my favorite yellow summer dress and the beach sandals Sheila had bought me when we went to Jamaica—alongside a bra and pantie.

I smiled in my mind—smiled at the consideration.

I climbed into the tub and soaked in the heated showers that massaged my muscles tenderly. It woke my body up. I washed, stepped out, and then moisturized. I grabbed my wide-tooth comb, which sat beside my clothes alongside my big hair pins, and styled my hair. I brushed my teeth with my Neem-oil toothpaste, applied deodorant, and dabbed a touch of natural rose and vanilla oil on my special places.

I didn't realize how much my sisters remembered my little personal needs and likes. They had made sure I had everything.

Exiting the bathroom, I walked down the hall with short, soft strides. I heard their voices—intentional whispers filled the air. So, I prepared myself again. Then finally, my slightly reluctant steps turned the corner and entered the kitchen.

There they were: Angel, Sheila, Samantha, and Purple—wearing faces of tender sensitivity. Seeing their faces was like seeing their beautiful souls. Immediately, the guardedness dropped and openness was. I saw their love through their consideration, which embraced my spirit so much that my petals started to open up slightly after two cruel-weathered nights.

In that moment, these nurturing beings were more than gifts to me—they were sunshine.

I was so happy they were there.

****

After I gathered myself from the mixture of emotions I was experiencing with the ladies at Purple's kitchen table, I started to share with them what happened—what had made me so wretched, so vulnerable, so hurt.

The ladies' eyes were intense and consumed—consumed with suspense that pressed their hands to their chests as I talked.

"Women, and a crazy woman. Rage. And crazy—where do I start? I know I sound mad," I said in bewilderment.

"Well, start with what happened after you left his office—after finding the letter and the panties," Angel said.

"Well, I guess that's a good place to start. After that incident, Daniel called me a couple of times that night—but I didn't answer. I was still upset and agitated. But he was persistent, calling me as early as five o'clock in the morning. I eventually picked up, and we talked briefly. He kept apologizing and then asked if I could be with him for the weekend while he was working—you know, promoting his new book and all. He said he wanted me by his side all weekend, and in the time between, we could talk about everything. So, I accepted. I knew we needed to sift this through.

That Friday evening, we met at *Young Cry*, the famous college radio show in the city. And time there is what sparked everything... Before the show, Daniel stepped out to meet me before going into the booth with the hosts. We had a rather short embrace, because the tension between us wasn't healed yet. As I walked down the hallway, I noticed a group of women cluttered in a corner waiting on him.

"One yelled, 'Can we take some selfies with you?!'

"Daniel nodded, giving them permission with his classic smile. Then the ladies ran over to him, pressing into his sides to capture their moment with him. I guess my face held sadness or something, because Daniel looked at me briefly with dented brows. Then he asked me to get in and said to the other women, 'The rest of the pics taken have to be taken with me and my fiancé.'

"My heart jumped for joy. I thought his gesture was so cute. I guess he wanted to sweep out any doubt or isolation I was feeling out the door. It seemed like briefly the ladies were going to turn down the offer with their brief, sharp looks at me, but instead, they rushed me into the pics with the sweeping of their hands. He held me at his side as we peered into the many phones. I felt included, and even though I knew those ladies wanted my man, it felt good having Daniel softly state that he was already taken.

"After all the pics were finished, one of the ladies I pressed into during the selfies, an orange-red haired woman who smelled like cough drops and cigarettes talked in a low-pitch to her friend.

'His fiancé isn't even that cute,' she said. It irritated me, but not as much as what came next."

Purple interrupted my reality TV.

35

"Opal, Hun, don't pay that girl no mind—you are beautiful."

All the ladies concerted in agreement.

"Ladies, it's okay… you all don't have to…" I stated. I knew the ladies wanted to speak positive energy into that negative comment I received. No woman—I don't care who she is—wants to hear that she isn't that pretty.

I continued.

"So, outside the booth, I sat and watched the interview. The hosts were young, engaging, and asked pretty solid questions—a lot of crazy questions too—but Daniel handled them effortlessly in his subtle Apologetic style.

"However, shortly after, the station went into a session they called 'Bring-It,' where he was responding to calls coming into the station. A question from a female came in. She asked him how he felt about being called the 'Hot Prophet.' She said it with an animated voice that jolted the girls behind me.

"They all started screaming, becoming this rambunctious rally that seemed to elevate with every word that lady spoke, and they participated rather exuberantly—like I wasn't even there. It gave me an uneasiness that made every part of me feel uncomfortable.

"After that question, Daniel became very flustered and smiled that killer side-smile, which revealed that dangerous shallow dimple—that dimple that causes knees to buckle.

"Before he opened his lips to speak, however, one young blonde girl, who could not have been more than twenty, ran out of her seat and screamed, 'I love you! I will do anything for you! You're my soulmate!'" (Between Angel, Sheila, Purple, and Samantha, grunts spouted, lips smacked, and eyes rolled—but I continued through their gestures.)

"My eyes were enlarged by this young girl's gall, and other eyes emulated mine and then those same eyes glued onto me from all sides of the room as they awaited my response. It seemed they wanted that loud stereotypical response. I almost felt obligated to go-off by their silent but resounding gazes. Then this...young..."

(I shook my head, pressing the words that needed to come out.)

"This young, poor girl lifted up her bra and smashed her breasts on the interviewer's glass."

An intruding thought: As I was telling my sisters about this, a memory from my youth flashed in my mind of a young girl exposing herself in front of a boy I adored. But the ladies gasps and grunts interrupted that image from long ago. I snapped back as Purple spoke.

"No, she didn't."

"Oh yes she did, those college girls will expose themselves in a minute," Angel said with twisted lips.

"Whaaat, like why? She knows he is a man of God!" Sheila responded.

"God save us, we are living in the last days," Purple responded.

"I'm sorry, I would have smacked that Heffa, she just gon' disrespect me like that and entice my man—all hecks naw," Angel interrupted.

"We need to pray for that baby, not smack her," Purple interrupted.

Angel started pacing back and forth as if the incident had happened to her. She started slightly turning red.

"Angel, sit down. Hitting that young girl will not be—love," Sheila responded. Then, as swiftly as Sheila said that to Angel, Sheila turned to me and said, "Opal—what did you do?"

The ladies looked at me with locked eyes, awaiting my next word, my next act. I continued.

"I quickly looked at Daniel—he quickly looked away from the young blonde—then he looked at me. He moved his lips through the sound-proof glass. I read them. *'I'm so sorry,'* he said. I then stood up and in a calm, but firm voice I said, "Young girl, can't you see I'm right here, please respect me and my fiancé."

"Classy," said Sheila.

"Naw, that's sad Mrs. O, you should have come a little harder than that," Angel responded swiftly.

Samantha sort of chuckled at Angel, but Purple stood silent.

I continued.

"My response seemed to agitate the whole room, like they wanted me to be more aggressive and throw chairs at that young girl or something, it's like the other ladies became very irritated the moment I stood up speaking calmly instead of hollering. So, I guess they felt they needed to bring what I didn't, because they all started to yell at her, like she caused them harm—it was weird.

"One lady sort of shoved her as if Daniel was her prize. Then it seemed like they started agitating each other and it became heated in the room—fast. Then, the young blonde girl screamed, 'I don't care what they say! We are supposed to be together!' And then this young girl had the nerve to be tearing up.

I remember looking into that young girl's eyes, they were stuck on Daniel, engulfed in infatuation. She was serious, determined—desperate—like she needed him to survive. Then suddenly, a group of young men ran into the room, full of ignorance and high hormones trying to witness the young girl exposing herself. The guards showed up and then I saw everyone around me go into this thick confusion and anger. There was no respect for Daniel's platform, book, or message of God he hoped to bring to the young generation—it was chaos, and this chaos manifested itself within a matter of minutes. Then one of the girls jumped right in my face. 'You ain't gonna do nothing?' she snapped."

"I said in my head...yeah, I'm going to do something. That girl was just the prompting I needed.

"Ladies, I stood up on one of those black plastic chairs in the viewing area, and I hollered—with everything in me, 'Every unclean spirit, every demonic spirit, LEAVE NOW in the name of JESUS!'"

Sheila butted in. "Oh, dear Lord, you went to church on them?" Angel shook her head.

Purple nudged Sheila giggling. "She went charismatic church too!"

I continued through their giggles.

"I said, 'I rebuke all unclean spirits in the name of Jesus! Lord Jesus—clear the room of each and everything that is not YOU!'

"Then suddenly...and yes, I mean suddenly... there was this silence, like a vacuum had sucked up all the noise. Instantly. And I believe Jesus was that vacuum who came in swiftly and glued every mouth and froze every, body—leaving roaming eyes, which followed me.

"The hosts in the booth, and even Daniel, were stuck looking at me. Maybe they thought I was crazy. I do not care what they thought, because, suddenly people stopped whatever they were doing and walked out slowly. Not even a whisper was left in the room.'

"Did that really happen Ms. O?" Angel said swiftly.

"Why would I make something like that up?" I responded.

"They thought you were craaaazy—that's why they stopped," Angel said with her eyes stretching and her face still in shock.

Sheila interrupted.

"They probably were like this lady stepping on chairs talking about Jesus and demons—they didn't know what was going on," Sheila said with a slight chuckle.

"Maybe at first, but even those with worldly eyes had to notice the halt in all that abnormal activity after a while," Purple responded.

"Yes, that's true," Sheila agreed.

"Then what happened?" Purple asked.

"Daniel walked out of the booth, grabbed my hand, and helped me down the now wobbly chair. I looked at him and tried to study the lines in his face, not knowing if I caused him any embarrassment. But he softly smirked and pressed me to his side and said with a deep undertone:

'I see you going to war out here—it indeed was a spiritual one.' Then he kissed me on my forehead. The host of the radio show blinked, seemingly coming out of his hold."

"That's crazy," Angel interrupted.

"That is," stated Sheila.

I nodded in agreement as I continued talking.

"Then Daniel knocked on the glass while still holding onto me and asked the host if he wanted to continue. The host agreed, and the end of the show was basically about what just happened."

(Before I continued, Pastor Chris broke into our world with his overreaching pastor voice.)

"It's time, ladies. You know the pastor can't be late."

"It was just getting good," Samantha said.

She'd been surprisingly quiet the whole time aside from her subtle gestures—I'm sure studying and dissecting each word that came out of my mouth.

"I guess I'll share it with you ladies later," I said.

Awwws… came out of the ladies in different tones and stretches. But we understood we had to go—Pastor Chris and Purple could not be late.

We composed ourselves in Purple's living room and then headed to our cars.

"O, you want to ride with me, or are you okay driving yourself?" asked Sheila.

"I'm not dying, Sheila. Hurting, but not dying," I chuckled.

Even though I said that, a part of me felt like I was dying without Daniel.

I started up the engine in my Honda, and it was like it sparked the engine in my mind to continue where I left off with the ladies.

Rewinding. My mind kept rewinding.

I thought about what happened next, and I was glad I was stopped by Pastor Chris. I probably would have spilled too much in my vulnerability. Some things Daniel shared with me were personal, and the ladies did not need to know them.

After that crazy scene, that crazy interview, Daniel and I went to get a bite of food. We were laughing and talking the whole time, spewing jokes about not being invited back to *Young Cry*—especially me. We laughed again, then we became serious and prayed about the whole experience there. The red pantie falling out of Daniel's book hadn't even come up yet. To tell you the truth, I didn't even want to talk about it anymore—it was just us, and I wanted to stay there. For a moment, ignorance was bliss. But staying there was hopeful wishing, because suddenly, Daniel gave me this sobering look. He became serious. The look transmitted from his consciousness to mine—it was time to talk.

Oh, oh, I thought.

I started bracing myself for another—My thoughts were cut off.

"Opal, the other day, I lied."

He said it quick and with force, like he was working up the courage to say it.

Lied—what!? A thought raced.

His words took the air out of my lungs for a second.

I hoped the lie was not—an actual affair. Not an actual thing. A romance of some sort that had him questioning me, *us*.

"The woman," he said.

Daniel threw up bunny ears with his fingers.

"Red Rain—I do, know her."

The drums of my heart quickened.

He continued.

"I was once in love with her. Tanya is her name. I did communicate and flirt with her like I do with you now—through books and such, because of the roles we had—but she is the only one."

Daniel's face exposed regret, and his movements revealed a slight nervousness.

"Tanya is a professor. She used to teach at the university I teach at now. And, yes, it was getting serious—we were about to be engaged. However, we never made it that far. The break-up was spiritual at its core—a silent battleground sprouted from the convictions, or should I say *non*-convictions, of our lives. Tanya wasn't as convicted in her faith as I thought, and she was always trying to seduce me—and we weren't one yet—not that I didn't want to. My past grumbled inside me often when I thought about sharing this with her—I am a flesh and blood man. But I am, of course, a spiritual man as well. I wanted to stay firm in my commitment to God, especially because of my past."

He paused. Then continued.

"However, it seemed that as time moved on, she became more assertive—very manipulative at times. Saying little nasty remarks. Acting as if something was wrong with me. Or maybe I was attracted to the same sex—she just couldn't understand why I wouldn't sleep with her—even though she knew I was trying to honor my faith.

Honor *God*. It's like her mind believed me, but her heart thought I was playing some sick game.

"I believe trying to be abstinent made her feel... unwanted. But I told her many times that I truly desired her. It just wasn't sinking in. And toward the end... she was becoming this whole new person."

He exhaled hard before continuing.

"One late night, when we were up watching a movie, she went into a room—then came back out... completely bare. I didn't know what to do. I told her to go put something on or I was leaving.

"She ignored me. Walked closer. And it's like I couldn't move. My flesh was taking over every part of my body. She seduced me and I became putty in her hands—I gave in. It's like I had no strength to fight. The next morning, I felt awful. I completely failed the oath. She took advantage of a craving I could not kill. I was an addict, in a sense... and she let out a well-known animal."

I swallowed hard after Daniel said that, wondering if he was going to say that this *Red Rain* was a problem—or if this was the lead-in for him to tell me that *this addiction* was going to be an issue.

I couldn't speak, I just listened, tongue paralyzed. Daniel continued.

"So, when that happened, it opened up old appetites. I was sexualizing everything as I once did before. I felt horrible, but it's like I couldn't stop myself—especially with her. I wanted her and I wanted it. My eyes wandered towards the ladies in my class, which my spirit will always stop, but now my spirit gave way too, because that spirt of lust hovered me and it was starting to consume me again. It inflamed in me, pulling out that relentless craving, and Tanya's body became my dose of heroin.

"When it came to her, I was weak—defenseless. I felt so convicted after a while that I just started looking for wedding rings—just to propose, so I could get out of guilt. I was not thinking about her manipulation, her indifference to God—my beliefs. Everything just felt wrong amidst the illusion of quick thrills.

"My clear weakness—she exploited. I was blinded by her beauty, the physical intimacy, and even the guilt I felt. So as a result, I was planning to propose. I was headed to Tanya's to do just that, but ironically, I ran into Kent, an old colleague, and meeting him stopped me in my tracks."

Daniel briefly paused. I was still on pause. I was covered in suspense, holding onto every word that left his mouth, I was even hanging onto the brief silence. Then he continued.

"I heard a voice behind me. 'Don't do it, she is not worth it!' Out of nowhere Kent said this, Opal. I turned around and saw that it was Kent and I asked him why he said that because he knew nothing of Tanya or any current events in my life—so it shocked me.

Again he said, 'Don't do it, she is not worth it!' I looked at him in bewilderment. 'She is not good for you.' I looked at him longer in wonder. He read my face and pointed at the car before us. 'The BMW you were staring at, the dean's car, you were looking at it like you were thinking about buying one for yourself. She is beautiful, but the upkeep will kill you. What dean has a car like this, anyway?'

"Kent was trying to make casual conversation; however, his words mirrored my situation exactly—speaking directly to every thought I'd had just moments before. In that moment, I knew it was Yahweh speaking through him, warning me not to get engaged. I told Kent I had to go. I left him and drove away, broken, in utter repentance and prayer. I was groaning, toiling in my spirit before God for at least five hours.

Then suddenly, I felt it. A breaking. A shattering. Deep in my spirit. It was like a flood rushed through my head, cleansing months of torment—lust, guilt, and the gripping fear of separation.

And then... His peace returned to me.

It was calm. Comforting. I had missed it.

I could finally see clearly again. I saw how I had been lusting after her all along, and when she pressed in hard, I was too depleted to resist. The truth? I let her wear me down." Daniel shook his head.

"I saw her actions, but ignored it—and as such, it dampened my strength. However, I started to see clearly again, I saw how she didn't really believe in or care about my convictions—only about soothing her insecurity, satisfying her appetite, and pursuing her agenda.

So instead of proposing that evening, I ended it—right there on her doorstep. I cut off the hand that was causing me to sin. To betray my own heart. To go against Yahweh."

I looked at him—deeply. Intentionally. Letting my eyes speak the message: *I understand.*

Funny thing is, I *did* understand. All too well.

That's what happens when Yahweh is calling you closer. I remembered the last guy I dated before Daniel. The moment I brought up abstinence, he left me—with no response—right there at the diner on our second date. And the look he gave me before walking away? Like I had an eye in the middle of my forehead.

The second guy I dated—before my long dating hiatus—seemed like the real deal at first. I told him upfront on our first date. I wasn't going to waste my time or his. He said he understood. And for a while, he acted like it—temporarily.

But after three or four months—and three or four *slick* attempts to seduce me—I had to shut it down. I remember that final moment so clearly: two adrenaline-filled legs pushed him straight against the wall. I think he really thought he could wear me down.

My shove said everything. It told me he wasn't the one and it told him he was never going to get to my sacred place. I still remember the shock on his face, I guess he thought that handsome face was going to penetrate the will of my heart. That is when I realized I wanted a man whose heart was like mine—after God's heart. This is where and when I asked God to open up my spiritual eyes. I can see how weird I was to that guy—it was all over him. Weird is always a thing when one does not understand a person or situation. That moment was the moment I really started to understand that scripture that says God's people are a peculiar people.

Daniel's voice began to pierce my memories—I had to snap out of it—Daniel was still talking—whoops. I began to latch on to his every word again.

"And... Tanya did not take the breakup well. She figured she would hook me again how she hooked me before. She started sending me provocative photos… and would place provocative things in my books in my office. It was like she was obsessed.

She said in one letter that being away from me was like a daily storm—she felt like rain every day. That I was the only true love she ever had, but that she also yearned for me sexually. *It was a red desire,* she stated. Consequently, until we reunited, that is what she called herself—*Red Rain.*

I thought I was able to handle her attempts, but at times, it became overwhelming. She can be so consistent and assertive. I had to admit—that part attracted me—and she knew it.

I eventually had to put a restraining order against her; that is how loud she was becoming. She started popping up at my home, at speaking engagements, and in class with my students—it affected our work. So much so, that it spilled its way over to the dean. As a result, I had to give him some of the new letters and material she sent me that week. Shortly after, Tanya was encouraged to find work elsewhere. The loss of her position seemed to be the thing that motivated her to finally leave me alone. I didn't hear from her for years after that—until a couple of days ago.

I am still trying to figure out how she was able to come into my room unnoticed to put that note and pantie in my book—or who could have even done it for her."

Daniel had this weird look of ambiguity on his face. When he stopped talking, his perplexed expression turned into concern, and it moved upon me through his heart-pressing eyes. He was awaiting my response. I looked at Daniel for a long second, undeterred. Then I spoke.

"Why did you feel like you had to lie to me?" I said with an extra twist in my neck. Daniel responded.

"I was ashamed of telling you this—my past and still present struggles. I was afraid of how you would look at me, and I also didn't want to seed extra things in your mind that aren't there."

Daniel's heart-pressed eyes became sorrowful.

"Please forgive me." He stated with a low… bass. That low bass moved my insides. I saw regret and shame, it formed in his whole body. His strong, erect frame sloped and sunk. I was still a little upset, but his vulnerability, I felt I could not betray. I embraced him and pecked him on his shallow dimple.

"Thank you for sharing this with me Daniel." Then looking into the center of his eyes, I said, "Don't be afraid to talk with me, we have to start with trust."

"I know," he responded.

After his words, I curled up into his large, muscular arms and heaved in relief. I was so at peace there, in his arms. We stayed in his truck for hours just talking, talking, and embracing until the skies exposed the stars above. Then eventually, we had to depart. We had to go to our separate homes. And we did. I wasn't totally sure how to place everything in my heart with Daniel that night on my way home, but I know it hurt leaving him. I wanted his home to be my home. I yearned to have his subtle woodsy aroma drape over me all night, I wanted to hear his calming voice put me to sleep. I wanted to enter into covenant. But exhaustively, it was not time.

I was still in my car pondering, rewinding in my mind as I turned my steering wheel, tailing the ladies to church. I thought about what Daniel shared with me—it sat with me and latched onto me like Velcro. It's funny—I thought that disturbing feeling would just vanish, and that the next evening would be a fresh start. Boy, was I wrong.

It was this evening that brought about the last straw… I did go from forgiving him to embracing him—then to running away from him within two days. My mind circled around, showing me the succession of events back-to-back that led to me running. From what happened at Young Cry to him sharing his weakness, then to the evening, the evening that added the last straw that led to my collapse. I processed the evening of the event all over again.

I was getting ready to attend the Elite Awards. I had the whole morning and afternoon to myself. Daniel had to meet up with some colleagues before The Elite Awards, so he was going to come pick me up later. He was actually going to be honored that night. As a result,

I made sure I did all my womanly pampering and beauty preps. I shaved and waxed, I masked my face and body, and arched my wild brows. I wanted to look perfect for Daniel that night—I wanted to be perfect. I wanted to start all over and go back into our world of awe for each other. I was determined to keep drama out and keep joy in.

Once I'd finished all my pampering, I slipped into a midnight-black chic dress that hugged every curve. I picked it up from Ama, my African sister who could recreate anything you saw on TV and make it personally yours. I then opened my jewelry box which housed my many treasures from some of my best vacation spots with my sisters. I selected a set of earrings I picked up in Spain with Samantha and Sheila. I put on the dangling crystal drops, a matching large crystal bangle, and a seemingly invisible crystal necklace that carried a unique crystal stone.

I decided to wear rouge lips and just a very subtle dash of rouge on my cheeks. No foundation, just a matted Shea butter finish to my skin. I put on my oils, different oils Daniel had not smelled on me yet, and I polished my nails rouge to match my lips. My hair, I elegantly French braided up in the back to allow my natural curls to poof up on top and hang on the side. I wanted to be on Daniel's arm as his prized jewel. I looked in my oversized mirror and said to myself, *Girl, you look good!*

Seven o'clock came around and I heard Daniel's strong knocks on my door. I opened the door slowly, trying to give some effect to the artwork I put together for him. As I opened the door, his eyes lit up like candles and my heart leaped from his response. He grabbed me by the waist instantly and kept telling me how beautiful I was in a slow reminiscent way while kissing my lips and my cheeks.

"I want to look like this every day for you," I said like a gullible teen.

"No, I'll miss you too much. Yeah this is special, we can do special for special occasions, but then there's just... you...your natural, native self, and that, I can't see myself without any day."

My heart started to hit Soprano notes as I dove into his lips again.

Knock, knock, knock. My mind fell back into the present moment. Knuckles rapped once more against my car window. Those knocks interrupted the movie going on in my head showcasing the recent past days with Daniel and me. It was Sheila. She was mirroring Purple the other day, waking me up from my pathological processing, which had taken me completely out of the present.

"Opal—are you okay?" Sheila asked in a concerned tone.

I came out of my space and again realized I had split minds carrying me, one part of my mind was driving to the church and tailing the ladies as we drove from Purple's house, the other part was watching a non-fictional camera-reel. Or was it even my mind carrying me at all? I rolled down my window.

"Yes, I'm fine," I said, as I looked into the mirror trying to collect myself and act as if I had been trying to get myself together the whole time. As I entered the church doors, I prayed a little prayer, to keep my thoughts at bay.

CHAPTER 5

*B*ack from church, I plopped down on my sofa. Church was good as always. I needed that Word. I slid the sandals off my feet and grabbed the remote control, which sat on the arm of my sofa. I clicked the home button, and the screen awakened. As the screen revealed the images, I noticed *Runaway Bride* was on—one of my favorite movies. When I saw Julia running away, I couldn't help but think about me running away from Daniel.

My mind circled back yet again, rewinding and rewinding... I guess I was trying to make sense of everything, process it all. I went back to the event before I was interrupted by Sheila's knocks on my window.

The Elite Awards event was a beautiful event. It was elegant and classy—my taste. I was enjoying myself initially, studying the people, especially the décor. I studied it like a scientist studying a new specimen. I wanted the name of the person who set up the event. Everything was so sharp—clean. It was an event indeed made for stars—they sure made you feel that way, anyway. Before Daniel and I entered, a couple of photographers took snaps of us and all of the incoming people. One beckoned Daniel to "give up the goods" on me—the new woman on his arm—as he snapped pictures as fast as lightning. And it was perfect timing, because Daniel and I were all over each other, the effects from our recent reunion. We were full of eyes that shared stories no one else knew, and chemistry that left sparks between our roaming hands. We were so googly-eyed—and we hadn't even consummated yet.

As the night went on, I noticed the event was consumed with intellectuals and their ideologies, and owners and CEOs, boasting about their accomplishments. Besides all the apparent prestige and puffiness that filled the room, Daniel and I were having a wonderful time enjoying each other. I saw how people looked at me as I molded to Daniel's side like I was an extra hip—it aroused their curiosity. They seemed fascinated with me—us. I could almost hear their thoughts: *Who is this woman with the Hot Prophet? Oh… she's a Black woman.*

The people there seemed amused by Daniel's choice—this spoke through their eyes as they lit up with hints of intrigue. They were looking at me the way Daniel looks at me sometimes, as if I were some exotic creature they hadn't seen before.

Daniel, the star, was like David Bowie, and I was his Iman. They combed over my frame with their busy eyes and, it seemed, placed their stamp of approval on me, validating me with winks and enchanting stares.

One of the leading conversations of the night was Daniel—the most wanted bachelor—being soon to be wed. It circled the atmosphere like Hollywood gossip. Funny thing—in this atmosphere, I saw different reactions from Daniel. One of them was him being jealous—and not me. And I witnessed this jealousy quite a few times. It was something to see, because Daniel was always so confident, sure, and unaffected.

But this night, I witnessed that—and a little extra.

When some of the gentlemen grabbed my hand to kiss it upon introduction, Daniel did not like it at all. I felt displeasure all in his body. His stirred energy bounced onto me, especially when this very attractive, smooth, dark chocolate man kissed my hand and then looked at me like he wanted to eat me. Daniel, smoothly and casually, took my hand and gently moved it from the fellow's lips. Then I saw him look at that African-warrior-looking gentleman with stern eyes I hadn't seen before.

There was an invisible, territorial aroma that vaporized off them that sort of made me uncomfortable. Seems like Daniel would have said something, but shortly after that, a great big man named Charles Appleton came into our circle with rosy, happy cheeks and Jack Daniel jolliness.

"This man is the man of the night!" he bellowed.

He brushed his hands over Daniel's shoulders in all of his 6'4 or 6'5 height—he had to be, because Daniel was 6'3, and Charles hovered over him slightly.

Charles had dusty blonde hair and rather odd features. His cheeks were big and round, but his eyes were small—they looked beady behind those gold-framed, 70s-style glasses. Maybe it was the strength of his prescription.

Besides his odd look, though, he seemed to be a cool guy.

I had met Charles at a gathering before with Daniel. Charles is a very successful owner of a skyrocketing software company, which Daniel was a key advisor for since its inception.

Charles tugged at Daniel's shoulders with happy arms. Then Daniel looked back at me with "help me" written in his eyes. I chuckled and waved goodbye, then swept the room to explore.

But my isolation didn't last long.

An austere-looking man with wonderfully silver hair came into my sphere. His face looked so much younger than all that silver surmounting his head and draping his chin. He also had silver eyes that matched his silver hair.

"Hello, Ms.," he said.

He had a thick accent.

"Hello," I responded.

"My name is Dr. Demitri Sokolov, but you can call me Demitri."

"Hello—Opal Cleverson," I said with a soft smile while shaking his hand.

"I understand you will soon be marrying Dr. Pacini—my archrival."

"Archrival? I didn't know Daniel had a nemesis," I said with a chuckle.

"You don't know?"

"No, I'm sorry—should I?"

"I debated Daniel a few times… about the existence of God."

As soon as he said that, I remembered a conversation Daniel and I had one late night under the stars about this Russian guy he told me he had debated at a couple of universities—and even on TV.

I remember him saying that this man was one of the fiercest people he'd ever debated—that he was tenacious. He said Sokolov seemed to grow fiercer with every response Daniel gave to his arguments. He said he was... very persistent, arrogant, and condescending.

I snapped out of my memory.

"Oh, yes, I do believe I remember Daniel talking about you— he said you gave him a hard time."

"I believe that's me. It's good to meet you," he responded.

I nodded. "And you."

"I believe I heard about your tenacity as well—at that young college station... Young Cry."

"You heard about that?"

"I believe a lot of people did, love."

"Okay…" I said slowly.

"Well, it certainly sounds like you and Daniel have the same heart."

"I certainly believe so."

Demitri started to chuckle. It was a creepy chuckle.

"Daniel intrigues me," Demitri said suddenly, with no rhythm.

"Welcome aboard. He intrigues a lot of people," I responded.

Demitri chuckled again.

"I find that he has this incomprehensible grip on this God he so worships... when he seems to have no need of God."

"Excuse me?" I said, wearing an intentional question mark on my face.

"He has everything going for himself—wealth, prestige, looks, beautiful women—and yet he chooses to submit himself to the rules of a being that was made to give poor or unfortunate people comfort."

Anger went up my back and wanted to fire off on this arrogant snoot who thought he knew everything—but knew nothing at all. He seemed hydrated, but spiritually dry. The man didn't realize that the science of his very being was wrapped in so much intelligence, it screamed *Creator*. But I extinguished the fire with a long sigh... and the thought of God's kindness. It seemed ears awaited nearby and bodies had begun to sneak up to listen.

I responded:

"Oh Demitri, you're confounded because you believe these worldly things of which you speak bring life and fulfillment—when indeed, it is God Himself who does. Daniel understands that. He has all these things you speak of in such a beautiful and elegant way because he's proven he can handle them—for his individual call and purpose in life, not for his self-glory. Daniel never buries his coin. You, sir, have made *these things* your gods... and that's why *his* God is foreign to you."

Demitri opened his mouth to respond—surely to launch into a full-on debate—but a man suddenly stepped into our space.

"Ouch! She told you, Demitri."

Demitri glanced at the man with those crude silver eyes.

"She told me *nothing!*" Demitri snapped.

The man's shoulders ignored him. Then he turned to me, extending his hand.

"I'm Heath Kingston," he said in a crisp British accent.

Heath Kingston was a very fair-skinned man with striking golden-blond hair, bright sea-blue eyes, and strong, square features. He looked like the quintessential Englishman. He had to be between forty and forty-five years of age.

"Opal Cleverson," I said.

Heath kissed my hand.

"I know. Pleased to finally meet you."

A memory struck.

"Oh... Heath—the groomsman I haven't had the pleasure of meeting yet."

"That's me," Heath replied.

He was one of Daniel's selected groomsmen I hadn't had the pleasure of meeting until now—mostly due to their clashing schedules.

"Well, hello," I said.

Demitri chuckled, clearly trying to recapture my attention. His face was irritated. In fact, it seemed he became uncomfortable with Heath's very presence. Suddenly, a swarm of fellows entered my circle with Heath, including that African warrior-looking man—the one who earlier exchanged that silent territorial moment with Daniel. He looked at Demitri like they had history.

53

"Demitri causing trouble again I see—always after Pacini," one of the men remarked.

"And why not? It's my duty to examine all things—as a professor, a researcher. That includes anyone. But you all treat Daniel like he's untouchable, like he's some kind of angel," Demitri replied.

"So... you *do* believe in angels," Heath quipped.

The men behind him erupted in laughter.

"Demitri, go have a drink—please," Heath snapped.

A voice bellowed from behind, "That's the *last* thing Demitri needs when he's talking about Pacini. He'll get so mad, he'll end up getting himself kicked out of this fine establishment."

"Well, that'll be better for us all," Heath responded.

They all started to laugh as their masculine tones filled the air. Demitri's body became severely agitated. He looked at Heath—whose face had suddenly turned serious—then turned to me. Demitri subtly bowed toward me, then leaned in.

He whispered: "For your protection... Daniel's weakness—*women.*"

My spirit twisted.

Demitri looked me straight in my eyes with those cold silver daggers of his—then left. Heath's eyes trailed him with upset brows. Then he turned back to me.

"What did he tell you?"

"Nothing really," I replied.

"He had a thing for Daniel ever since Tanya left him for Daniel," one of the men called out, puffing a thick burgundy cigar. "It has nothing to do with religion," he said to Heath.

Then another spoke. "No—it was the debates. He couldn't handle defeat. Tanya came afterward."

Tanya? Wait... Red Rain? My thoughts raced.

Heath dove back in. "All of you ignore that joker. He's an intelligent guy, but—hold up, is he?"

The men burst into laughter again.

Another man chimed in, "Pacini surely exposed him."

After the chuckles settled, Heath looked at me. "No, we're kidding, but sometimes it seems he can't control himself. And because of that, he disqualifies himself every time."

The other fellows gave sobering chuckles and nodded. I sort of nodded with them, but I found myself holding onto what Demitri said and what that man said, bringing up that woman, that Tanya, who I found out yesterday was Red Rain. Thoughts rushed through my brain: Why would Demitri tell me something like that... *That was not professional at all...*

I reflected some more and then another thought emerged... *Daniel's weakness is women...*

I remembered what Daniel confessed—the addiction. A disruption began to stir in my spirit. I was getting agitated. I quickly quoted Scripture in my mind to resist the thoughts: *The devil comes to steal, kill, and destroy.* I whispered internally, *I reject him.*

Then I repeated Philippians 4:8: *Whatever is true, whatever is noble, whatever is right, whatever is pure, whatever is lovely, whatever is admirable—if anything is excellent or praiseworthy—think about such things.*

I repeated the verse silently for about a minute, right there in the middle of that conversation with the fellas. I forced my mind to remember good, beautiful things—precious moments in my life. And slowly, those negative tensions faded. Then, at least for that moment, I was able to rejoin the men with a clear and receptive mind.

After some time, I found myself in a very interesting and even pleasurable conversation with the guys. But I noticed that many of their wives were no longer present, so I scanned the room and spotted groups of women scattered about—or linked arm-in-arm with their husbands or partners for the evening. I took that as my cue. Maybe having such long conversations with the men wasn't exactly customary in this space—or at least not for this long.

I readied myself to excuse myself, but before I could, Daniel came out of nowhere, parting the sea of men around me—territorial again.

"Hey guys, your wives—over there," he said, pointing to the far right, then to the left.

"You have a good one here, Daniel," Johnny said.

"Yeah, take care of this one," Jake added.

Take care of this one, I thought.

Then Old Aric—what the fellas called him—chimed in, "You found her."

Another patted Daniel on the back.

"If he cuts up—remember me," said Frank with a wink.

If he cuts up? I thought.

Daniel shoved him playfully and said, "You ol' dog," since Frank seemed to be one of the elder statesmen of the group. I'd managed to gather most of their names—young and old—and skimmed over their personalities in the short time we'd shared. Then Marco—the beautifully dark chocolate, African-warrior-looking man—said, "It was a pleasure."

Daniel glanced at him, and it seemed like even Marco's voice agitated him. Then Heath leaned in and whispered something in Daniel's ear. From Daniel's swift look across the room toward Demitri, I knew exactly what Heath had shared—Demitri's shenanigans.

Daniel nodded, then returned to my side and wrapped his strong arm around my waist.

"Gentlemen," he said, excusing us with a graceful exit. They all nodded to me and Daniel as we left their circle. We made our way around the room, chatting and laughing with many. We also engaged in quite a few insightful conversations that opened my eyes to a whole new level of networking in the business world. I thought to myself—hey, this night was good for me too, even though it was Daniel's moment, not mine.

Daniel was being honored with the 2018 Most Influential of the Year Award. There were other awards, of course—awards that everyone already knew they were winning. No surprises there. I guess that's what made them show up wearing million-dollar smiles. According to Daniel, this event was held annually for entrepreneurs and leaders. But it wasn't just about trophies—it was a night of major deals and high-level connections. This night was business.

Daniel believed part of his calling was to reach this particular group—leaders, inventors, and influencers of our world. And they were all there. Not just CEOs, but top professors, judges, analysts, architects, philanthropists, and major media heads. Amazingly, a good number of these people had been touched by Daniel's teachings, advice, or involvement in their companies and ventures. It was beautiful to witness.

Charles took to the stage, which was adorned with some of the most elegant and uniquely designed balloons I'd ever seen—giant, translucent spheres filled with gold and white shimmer. I was taking notes. I needed to know who made those balloons.

Daniel nudged me gently out of my zone. He saw I was slipping into event-planner mode again. I chuckled a bit, and then looked to the stage after I took a couple of pics of the balloons on my phone.

Then there was Charles—on stage with gladness in all his limbs. He walked straight to the soloist and grabbed the mic with such authority, it seemed to slightly irritate the singer. It was a little rude, honestly—but I don't think he meant it. He just seemed overly excited. Probably because he knew he was about to grab the Most Successful of the Year Award. He was also one of the night's hosts. Charles started spewing off jokes, holding nothing back. A little raw at times—but hilarious. After his flurry of one-liners, a tall, slender woman emerged from the side of the stage to dramatic Oscar-style music. She looked to be in her mid-thirties, She had on a long, black, sparkly gown that the lights in the room danced on. She held a cream card in one hand and what looked like the first award in the other—a shooting crystal star.

Charles grinned with his beady eyes and took the cream card from her. Then he began to read. The room slowly dimmed, and the Elite Awards logos that had lit up the corner screens all night faded into fast-paced cinematic reels—footage of past winners filled the space like a theater premiere. The sound richly wrapped around us.

Charles bellowed, "The first award, the Rising Star Award, goes to... Marco Umbuntu!"

The screens were consumed with images of Marco's achievements over the past year. Thunderous applause broke out.

Hey, I know him—well, just met him, I thought. It was that attractive, warrior-looking guy.

Marco weaved through handshakes and back-pats, his radiant white smile gleaming from his beautiful brown skin as he approached the stage.

I could feel Daniel's eyes on me—checking to see if I was marveling.

But I didn't want him. I loved my Daniel. But it seemed like Daniel had an extra sense when it came to Marco. Maybe he felt there was some competition. Marco was tall and fit, with sharp cheekbones and a chin that made him look like the king of Wakanda. And he was very intelligent—articulate too. I picked up on that during our conversation earlier with the other fellows. However, Daniel must've known some back story about him other than him thinking I was attracted to him, because he seemed to be very bothered by him, that's for sure.

The night rolled on. Heath won the Most Prestigious Award. Charles followed, earning the Most Successful of the Year Award. And then, they called up my sweetie, Dr. Daniel Pacini—for the Most Influential Award.

He walked to that stage with such gentlemanly grace, it enlarged my awe. He thanked our Heavenly Father for the platform to influence and uplift others, then publicly honored me as his gift from God—his completion. I was so proud. My cheeks were raised and aching—I couldn't stop smiling.

Then Frank—yes, the same one who told me to call him if Daniel ever messed up—won the Lifetime Beacon Award for his years of contribution to business and commerce.

Right after the awards, the live band started to play Al Green's "Let's Stay Together."

"Finally, some soul," I said with relief.

Daniel chuckled. "I know."

He extended his hand and beckoned me to dance. He pulled me close, wrapping both arms around my waist.

Was there anything this man couldn't do? I thought as he swept me across the floor.

As we danced, I leaned in and said softly, "So… I met Demitri."

Daniel rolled his eyes, they spoke volumes, saying things his Christian lips would not utter.

"Yeah, I wanted to ask you about that, Heath told me about it somewhat."

"Well, he told me, he was your archrival and that he couldn't understand why you needed God and oh yes—your weakness."

Daniel shook his head.

"I can always expect Demitri to say something about my faith, but I'm curious what he states is my weakness—you?"

"No."

"Hmm."

"Well...I guess sort of kind of."

"What did he say it was, I'm curious?"

"It's a secret—he whispered it in my ear."

Daniel looked at me with confused eyes.

"You're not going to tell me?"

"Not right now."

"Okay...Did he say anything that offended you or hurt you—seduced you?"

I paused briefly, then spoke.

"It made me wonder, that's for sure."

"Hmm."

"But we will discuss it later, tonight is your night, don't let the enemy steal, kill, or destroy it," I said, alluding to the scripture I had to meditate on earlier. I said this, looking centered into Daniel's jewels. Daniel smirked and pressed me closer. He kissed me on my curls on the front of my head. "This is why I love you," he whispered.

The night went on and the rest of the party was fabulous. People were leaving, but Daniel, Heath and a couple of other fellows and their wives decided to stay in the restaurant in the back of the event for a quick late gathering of some sort. So, I decided to go freshen myself up.

"Daniel, I'm going to the ladies' room to freshen up."

Daniel kissed me.

"Okay, I'll be in the back, with the rest of the guys—this won't take long."

"Okay".

I headed to the ladies' room.

Humorous lady chatter, spontaneous laughter, and exotic perfumes floated through the air. Naturally, after freshening up and reapplying my rouge, I found myself chatting and laughing too—intermingling with different women. The ladies complimented me on my dress and how beautiful I looked. Then they asked, in so many different ways, how Daniel and I met—as if they didn't quite believe the story.

Then one of them, whom the other ladies seemed to snarl at to some degree (in their own vicious female way), spoke. She entered our conversation with a remarkable enthusiasm that left many of the other women rolling their eyes. The woman was a stunning beauty—so beautiful I almost felt intimidated. She had long blonde hair and emerald green eyes. She had clearly tanned before the event, because her skin glowed perfectly against her golden hair. She wore a beautiful chiffon dress that clung to her slim, model-like figure.

She kept saying how lucky I was to have snatched up Daniel. I smiled and said, "I feel blessed to have him."

The rest of the ladies gradually left, but I lingered in the restroom for a bit longer, texting Sheila about the event and responding to her hilarious pics of her kids and dogs—who were completely covered in flour across their floured kitchen floor.

When I was done texting, I noticed that the blonde beauty was still there—with me. Seamlessly, we started having a deeper conversation about men. She told me she was there to reunite with her true love—the one she hadn't seen in two years. I was elated for her and asked if she'd seen him already.

"Yeah. He's here… but with another woman."

I frowned.

"I'm sorry."

"How did you two split?" I asked.

"I broke it off because of his women, but I realized it was just me all along—so I'm here to get him back."

"Well, I wish the best for you," I said in a hopeful breath.

"It will be fine… he can't get enough of me. He told me there could never be another who could replace me. I felt like he didn't want me, so I left—but I shouldn't have. Now I can see that he was genuine… It took me some years to understand that."

"I hope you're right."

"I know it—we are soul mates."

I thought… *Soul mates—that word again.*

Then I started to think about her surety—she knew she was getting her man. But hey, she was beautiful and determined. I genuinely wanted the best for her and the guy.

As we exited the restroom, we shared smiles and then she walked away. But then—she turned her head back toward me, like she was posing for Vogue, and I gave her a playful thumbs up.

She rushed back to me.

"I'm sorry," she said, "I didn't catch your name. It was so lovely talking to you."

"Opal Cleverson."

She shook my hand and said, "Red Rain."

What?—my brain flinched.

I snatched my hand away from her as quick as wind.

"Excuse me?"

"Red Rain," she said again, this time with an insincere smile that turned slowly devious.

She knew I knew. She'd been playing me the whole time.

My heart sunk. Breathing stopped. Betrayal raged. Anger climbed.

I looked at her and shook my head.

"I should have known," I said. That chiffon dress was scarlet red, draped with a red sheer scarf.

When she turned swiftly around like a cheerleader in a snit, she swished away as if she were walking down a catwalk.

She's too beautiful, I thought. *What does she mean, she left him?*

Questions swirled in my head.

Daniel's addiction. Demitri saying Daniel's weakness is women. All the women throwing themselves at Daniel. The man who said,

"Take care of this one!" The young girl at Young Cry—And now this *Red Rain* mess.

War was present in my spirit, and fear revealed its ugly head yet again.

I went back to the restroom to get a gasp of air—to hide the arching of my back and the shattered anger on my face. I took a couple of minutes… and more than a couple of inhales and exhales.

I processed the past few moments and thought about all the drama—it's *always* about women.

I didn't know if I could do this.

Every day felt like a fight for my man. A restless anxiety. A worry that surrounded me, choked my peace, and buried it.

I loved Daniel. But was I ready to deal with this for the rest of my life? What about as I aged? As my body changed through possible babies? And… what if he *still* had this weakness with women and he rejected me for another? It would kill me.

I looked in the mirror and composed myself once again. I knew I had to go back out there. I opened the door slowly and walked into the back room as composed as I could.

The room only had a few people left—maybe eight, tops.

I turned to my left.

And there it was.

That red dress… hovering over Daniel.

She was hugging him in a way that sent lightning up my spine.

Then I looked at Daniel… and how he looked at her.

It seemed like he almost couldn't handle what was before his eyes.

Tanya—Red Rain.

The look in his eyes… I didn't like it.

As I looked further, my eyes captured another shade of red on him—and not just from the hovering of her dress.

My eyes zoomed in. It was red lipstick. On his collar.

That was it! Whatever composed face I had mastered in the restroom fell apart. I started to walk across the room with big, marching band stomps—as fast as I could. And it was like Daniel sensed the storm coming towards him and immediately his eyes flew towards me. He looked into my eyes as my force strode in his direction, and I realized he had a new look in his eyes: fear.

He tried to smile, but his face became awkward—like he was housing many emotions. That Tanya—that *Red Rain* woman—saw Daniel's face directed toward me, and she hugged him again. This time, Daniel pulled her long, tanned arms away.

As I came closer, I raised my voice in a tone that made it clear I had forgotten what establishment I was in.

"Excuse me, Red Witch—get your hands off of him!"

The attention of the room surrounded us.

"Ooh… Daniel, that doesn't seem quite graceful to me," she responded with a sly chuckle.

I tried to move toward her.

I wanted to punch her Vogue face.

Then Daniel grabbed my arm.

"Opal—calm down," he said in a firm undertone.

I was floored that he told *me* to calm down when *she* was the one draping herself all over him. I wanted *him* to tell *her* to calm down. I looked at him in subtle shock, and then I looked at Tanya's face—housing a twisted grin.

"I'm sorry, is this a game to you?" I belted.

"One I'm going to win," she responded.

"Opal, don't listen to her," Daniel said. "Tanya—whatever that was… what we had—that's over."

I smirked back at her with an intentionally lifted brow.

Then Daniel grabbed my arm, and we headed toward the table where Heath and Jake were. But Tanya flew in front of us.

"You didn't give me my goodbye hug," she said, using a kitten pout while giving Daniel this sexual stare that made my skin crawl.

I couldn't believe this woman—*who does this? She was too extra!*

I looked at Daniel. It seemed like he was internally fighting.

When I looked again at her twisted face—it *inflamed me.*

I ran and pushed her.

I pushed her so hard she stumbled into a high table full of bottles and glasses of wine. They tipped over, splattering wine all over Heath, Jake, and his wife. But Red Rain didn't fall. She had amazing balance in those high inch heels—which made me even more *livid*. She composed herself, then said, "Wow… Daniel, is she really someone you can take to an establishment like this?"

I was blowing red and black smoke, but something nudged me to scan the room—so I did.

Yikes. I saw the aftermath of my loss of self-control: spilled wine on people, unwanted stares, fortified stereotypes, and Daniel's big night tainted by my meltdown. Thank God there were only eight people left in the room… but still. I was supposed to be perfect for him tonight.

She set a trap for me—and I fell into it.

She stood there like the victim, acting like I was the perpetrator. Like she needed to be saved from *me*. I looked at Daniel and saw the embarrassment in his face.

I couldn't take it anymore—I darted out of there.

CHAPTER 6

*D*ays later, my lips quit moving as I finished telling my sisters the things that had been rewinding in my head from the past few days. I updated the ladies on everything—from Young Cry again, to the event, to Dr. Sokolov, to Red Rain.

The only thing I did not share with them was the secret Daniel had confided in me about his past sex addiction. After I explained everything, the ladies remained quiet for a moment. Then the silence was broken.

"Opal, you have to come to the reality that your fear and insecurity is bigger than your love for Daniel." Samantha's words clutched my throat—it was just out of nowhere.

"Is that a fair assessment? Everything she told us is a lot, and not her fault," Sheila commented in my defense.

"Samantha, how could you say something like that?" I responded.

"Why else would you leave him? He didn't leave you, remember—you said you broke it off—for what you were feeling from all these women—and this Red Rain woman… when he actually didn't do anything. Don't get me wrong, it *is* a lot. A lot of women would righteously feel what you feel, but you have to come to the conclusion that what broke you two up was your *feelings*… your feelings of fear and insecurity—and not his deeds."

Sheila intervened. "Well, the drama is sort of coming from him."

"But is the breakup *really* because of him?" Samantha emphasized with a slight elevation in her voice. The women remained quiet. The dead silence confirmed their contemplation.

"So, all of this is my fault then?" I said with an extra attitude.

The ladies were not affected by my pout—except Sheila, who looked at me with sympathetic eyes. Samantha interrupted those eyes.

"The women—no. The ending of a feasibly rich relationship—yes." Samantha said, turning the blade in my chest.

The other ladies... still silent.

I felt this growing anger taking over me. I raised up with a bark in my voice, while I picked up my purse to leave. "What about my feelings? They don't matter? I have to be attacked by women almost every day—and I guess you ladies too?" I snapped.

Sheila tried to console me. "Opal, we are not trying to say that at all—" Samantha interrupted.

"Sheila, stop babying her. Opal, sit down. The thing is, you are too much in your feelings—especially right now. You can't even hear what I'm trying to say to you."

"Maybe it's the way you're saying it," stated Sheila, directing a raised brow at Samantha.

"Ummhmm," Purple grunted.

Samantha looked at the ladies, then looked back at me. She hushed her tone a bit.

"Opal, you know I love you—we love you. And we are here for you. As your friend, your sister, it is my duty to be authentic and speak the truth, even if you don't like me the next day. So, I am being *me* for *you*. Please... sit down."

I tapped my feet while tears flushed down my face. I wanted to leave in my feelings—she was right. I wanted to be angry so I wouldn't have to face what she had to say. To face that, possibly... she was right. That maybe... I stepped out on Daniel too soon.

"Opal, please sit," Samantha repeated.

"Come on, Ms. O," Angel stated.

"Opal, you know we love you," Purple said, rising to stand beside me.

I sat down slowly when Purple chimed in. It was darn near impossible to resist her motherly spirit. So, I swallowed my pride. Samantha dove right in—with no reservations. "Let us look at this practically. Everything you told us was done by other ladies, not Daniel. When the ladies at the radio station tried to get your man in the photo—he included you. When that young thing pressed her twenty-year-old breasts against that glass, he turned away and apologized to you through the glass. He grabbed you by his side and believed in you when others did not—when you were going to war spiritually. When those men swarmed around you, you saw his fiery jealousy for you. When that Red Rain mess draped over Daniel, you said it looked like he was internally fighting—but he chose you. He pulled her arms away and told you not to listen to her, and that it was over. He has his pictures of you in the rooms he lectures in—to let women know he belongs to *you*. When you took off out of the establishment, you said he dashed after *you*. And now he's been lighting all our phones up, looking to see if you're alright—a week after you haven't responded to him once—the fight was around Daniel—but not Daniel!" Samantha belted.

Then an awkward silence manifested. Everyone knew Samantha was right—including me.

"Samantha, sometimes that judge-mind of yours gets on my nerves," I said with a sigh.

"Mine too, Ms. O, but she's right—like she is ninety percent of the time," Angel said.

"Ninety-eight percent of the time," Samantha said with a smug grin.

"Ar-rro-gant," said Sheila.

"She knows she is," said Purple.

Purple added, "It's not so much Samantha's judge-mind—which is trained to see through the mess and fluff—it's her simply being outside of the situation. Because of that, she can see through it clearly. *You're* in it, so your emotions are clouding your vision. But this can be any one of us on any given day—that's why we need each other."

"That's true," Sheila agreed.

"I must admit I'm afraid," I said. "I think the reality that I love Daniel so much scares me. So much so, that rejection from him scares me even more. So why not beat him to the chase? I look at him sometimes and I believe that I'm not good enough for him. He's better looking than I am—smarter. It's like I'm waiting for him to figure it out himself and finally leave. The ladies are a reminder of that."

"First—you are enough, Opal. You are beautiful, Opal—inside and out. That's why Daniel loves you. I believe you are attaching him to your past experiences. The people who left you—your mates, your biological father—they were not complete. They were lost and broken, and they imparted that brokenness to you. *It was never you.* But in all of this, I believe Daniel is real. He is the perfect man for you, Opal. He makes you happy, Opal. *Lighting the soul* happy. That is joy—and I want that for you," Samantha belted.

"I'm pathetic," I stated.

"Hush that," Purple responded.

"Opal, you're not—you're human," Samantha said gently.

Purple interceded again. "Remember, love… this is a *spiritual war*. The opposition exploited this—through all these crazy turns of events these past weeks—to try to get this very thing to happen: you and Daniel's breaking. The enemy does not want your joy, Daniel's joy, and especially the two of you coming together to do your *unique ministry*. Do you understand?"

Warm tears started to flow down my face again as Purple talked. I nodded in agreement.

"I've had enough of this. Satan, you won't win this one," Purple said with a growing anger.

Purple stood up and put her hands on my head and started to pray ferociously. I could feel the other ladies' hands pressing against my back, one by one, as she prayed—then she *shouted* at me. It seemed that shout electrified my system—like an AED. It certainly went right to my heart.

"Know who you are! Psalm 139:14—God said you are fearfully and wonderfully made! Joshua 1:9—Opal, hold onto it! Be strong and courageous—do not be afraid; do not be discouraged, for the Lord your God is with you wherever you go! Understand, Opal— you are validated, you are wanted, you are the daughter of the Most High God!"

Her words felt like compressions on my chest.

"Knowing this gives you your peace—no matter what happens. Feelings are fleeting. We don't want anything that is fleeting. We have Who is everlasting—and that is God Most High. Jehovah-Jireh!"

Her tone amped up.

"Proverbs 3:5–6—Trust in the Lord with all your heart... and do not lean on your own understanding. In all your ways, acknowledge Him, and He will make straight your paths."

Purple's voice thundered.

"2 Timothy 1:7—For God has not given us a spirit of fear, but of power... and of love... and of a sound mind. *Do you agree, Opal?!*"

Overwhelmed with storms of emotion—I exploded. "I agree!" I shouted, as tears raged down my shaking cheeks. Purple said, "Repeat after me." So, I did.

"I only walk in the fear of the Lord. That means I fear nothing and no one else."

I repeated. "I only walk in the fear of the Lord. That means I fear nothing and no one else."

"Because I am His, I will walk in power—not fear."

I repeated. "Because I am His, I will walk in power—not fear."

"I will let God's divine discernment and wisdom guide me—not feelings, which change like the wind." I repeated. "I will let God's divine discernment and wisdom guide me—not feelings, which change like the wind."

Then her voice hushed into a marvelous, deep calm. "So even if man fails me—I know God won't." I repeated. "So even if man fails me—I know God won't."

"Amen," Purple declared. All the ladies and I concerted together, "Amen."

The ladies huddled around me in one group hug. I felt their love pressing through their arms. When I opened my eyes, my vision was temporarily distorted from the puddles they contained, but as I blinked, I saw the others' tears joining mine.

CHAPTER 7

I was nervous about calling Daniel. I had completely shut him out this past week. I knew he had been trying to contact me—my sisters told me, and the slew of voicemails under his number confirmed it. I probably would've had a wave of texts too, but I had turned off all notifications. I didn't want any extra noise. I needed the solace found in silence. But now, that season of silence had passed. It was time to reach out again—to face Daniel and see where we stood.

I took my phone off vibrate and started to dial. But just as my finger hovered over the call button, the screen lit up—a call was coming in.

Wow. That was quick.

I didn't recognize the number, but I had been off the grid all week. It could be important. I picked up.

"Hello?"

"Hello," a sensual voice answered.

"I'm sorry, I'm not sure who this is—I didn't recognize your number."

"Thanks for picking up." Her voice sounded familiar...

"It's Tanya," the voice said.

"What—how did you get this number? You know what—it doesn't even matter right now." I was just about to press end when she shouted, "Please don't hang up—help me, please!"

Her plea stormed through the phone.

My finger hovered just a millimeter above the screen, but *help me* lingered in my spirit. Those two words were always hard to ignore.

"What do you want—and how did you get my number?!"

"Daniel is in danger—and I have something to give to you for him. He won't talk to me."

When she said this, every part of my body stood still.

"How do you know this—and how can I even trust you?"

"I love Daniel too."

Although her words took me back in my chest, I recognized a chord of authenticity. But I was still so very irritated and skeptical.

"I'm sorry for the other night."

I heard a crackling in her voice, I heard fright. My mind danced between anger, irritation, and curiosity. I was quiet.

"Are you still there?" she asked.

"Yes. I just… I don't know what you want me to say or do, Tanya."

"I have something Daniel needs."

"Ok."

"Can we meet up?"

I became silent again. I was trying to think—but my thoughts were not calm enough to answer clearly and reasonably. Tanya must have read my disposition.

"Please," she said. "If I had another way, I'd take it. But Daniel's truly in danger."

My voice belted out freely like water. My emotions spoke for me.

"When and where?"

"As soon as possible. You can choose the place."

"Well, I'm headed to work shortly. Maybe tomorrow, if you're in the city."

"Perfect."

"Are you familiar with Regis Park?"

"Of course."

"Then I'll meet you there—tomorrow at nine."

"Sounds good."

I hung up.

I sat for a second, stunned. How did she even get my number? I am going to have to drill that in when I see her—if I see her—But how can I not if Daniel is truly in danger? Then my thoughts raced.

What danger could Daniel possibly be in? I didn't know if I could trust that woman.

I grabbed my phone again and dialed Daniel. No answer. Straight to voicemail. I didn't leave a message. I wasn't even sure what to say. I hung up.

When I got to work, my assistant April was waiting for me in the lobby. Something was up—we never talk business there, and she never waits for me like that. Still, it felt good to see her—to return to work, even in the midst of emotional storms. I loved what I did: designing and creating events. It was my creative release, my sacred outlet in both the highs and lows. And April—April was the Godsend who helped me through them creatively.

April looked like the spring month itself. She is a brunette with bright green eyes and short in stature. She keeps her hair in these fun, short curls which she sweeps back on the side with a flower pin of some sort. April has cute button features that deceives people into thinking she was ten years younger than what she actually was. She is adorable and the best assistant in the world—anyone would love to have her. She was waiting for me with a beautiful smile, standing there with her huge tablet.

As I looked at April, I realized I had a great team around me. People that uplifted me and corrected me in love if need be for my betterment, like Samantha had the other day. I loved my sisters. I needed them so much during this time. After the conversation and prayer the other day with my sisters, I knew something changed within me, a moving of a sort, a shifting. However, for some reason, something still lingered. My sister's prayers brought me to the door of that lingering thing—but that lingering thing did not want to budge. It was a deep root that had ingrained its branches within my heart—my sisters had yanked at it—exposed it, but it did not want to come out. It still needed something… something more to finally let go.

It was as if my mind knew what to do, but my emotions hadn't caught up. My will was still holding on. I quietly asked the Lord to give me His strength in my weakness. Then I lifted my head and readied my mind. It was time to enter work.

I walked into the tall glass building where *Affinity* resided— my second home and business baby. Spinning through the revolving doors, I walked up to April who I saw waiting just beyond the glass. Something was definitely up. Excitement and concern danced in her fidgety movements.

"Hello Queen," I said.

"Hello Queen," she responded warmly.

"How are you—feeling better?" April asked.

"I'm feeling better now," I replied.

"Well, I knew it had to be something, because *Opal*, you never call off. I'm usually the one trying to send you home."

I looked at her with a little nod. She was right; colds, a broken arm from falling off a balcony one year doing an event, teeth being pulled, monster headaches, and even food poisoning didn't keep me from going to work. Little did she know, Daniel did. His absence took the wind right out of my lungs.

"So, what's up?" I asked her with a subtle curiosity.

April jumped in. "I know you said no business downstairs, but I had to warn you. There's a *fleet* of people waiting for you upstairs. I've been calling and texting all morning, but you didn't answer. I was getting worried. Then five minutes ago, I saw you park—so I rushed down."

"Warn me? Who are these people?" I became nervous. I also felt a flush of embarrassment at my own stubbornness—my texts had been off all week. And this morning… I had forgotten to turn the ringer back on.

I reached for my phone, switching notifications back on while simultaneously apologizing.

"I'm sorry, April. I had a feeling something was brewing. Do you know why they're all here?"

"It sounds like you made quite the impression with Daniel last week—and it stirred up some curiosity about your work." April handed me her oversized tablet, scrolling with a few swift motions. Then she paused and turned the screen toward me.

There it was—*The Golden Reader*, one of the most popular news outlets around. On the front cover: a photo of Daniel and me. The headline?

THE HOT PROPHET IS FINALLY TAKEN.

I did not care for the title, but the pose they caught was amazing. It made us look like we were young royalty—that visual team really knew how to work the article. My eyes raced across the fluffy language. They even listed my profession and place of work.

We did have to sign a release at the beginning of the event, allowing them to publicly post pictures across various media platforms. It was standard—meant to help promote the event and its attendees—but I didn't expect *this* kind of exposure.

"No way," I whispered in shock.

"Yes, Opal," April replied with a knowing grin.

"How many people?"

"Like thirty."

"Are there cameras up there or anything like that?"

"I don't think so, but you know folks always have their phones."

I turned and looked at her with wide eyes. "You're right."

We stepped into the brass elevator, and as the doors slid closed, I checked my reflection and fussed with my hair.

"You look great—don't worry," April said kindly.

"Thank you, April."

"Of course."

She pressed the number 5 on the panel and we began our ascent.

"Let's stick to our set appointments," I said. "I'll greet the visitors with a quick word—but we'll keep it brief."

"Remember—it's Monday. First half of the day is…"

"Creative space," we chimed together.

From eight to noon every Monday, we blocked out our calendars for what we called *creative space*. No appointments, no admin. Just ideation, fresh design concepts, and research on new materials and vendors. Unless we were massively behind on a project, it was sacred.

Ironically, this interruption might be happening on the most convenient day possible.

"I'll see as many people as I can until noon—first come, first serve. Then we'll schedule appointments for anyone willing to come back later," I said.

April nodded. "Your last appointment for the day rescheduled."

"Well, then plug someone in—whoever's willing."

As the elevator doors opened, I stepped out and was met with a lobby full of people. Every head turned my way, eyes sparkling, faces beaming like I had done something truly remarkable.

Weird. To my surprise, I recognized at least sixty percent of them from the Elite Awards. I turned on a polished smile and stepped into the crowd. "Wow... what is this?" I asked, matching their enthusiasm. One woman stepped forward, elegant and striking. She looked to be in her early sixties. She had big, gorgeous white hair that bounced around as she talked. Her makeup was flawless, and she was dressed in an amazing beige suit.

"I'm Diana," she said, beaming. "We haven't met, but I heard about your stunning presence at the Elite Awards, so I *had* to come see you for myself." She waved at the others I recognized from that night. "And we saw your fabulous work in the paper."

Then she leaned in closer, "And what you did to Tanya that night—we heard about it." She pulled back, locked eyes with me, and gave a sly wink and a thumbs up. Alot of us have history with her.

My face became embarrassingly awkward, I felt it. *Word gets around fast,* I thought. A few others from the group started chiming in—some familiar from that restroom gathering.

"We just wanted to come arrange dates with you—we've all got events," one lady said.

"Dinners," added another.

"Weddings... birthday parties..." someone else offered.

"And funerals," piped a short, dark-haired woman.

Diana brought it home: "And we want *you* to do them."

I smiled back and told them I'd love to. Then I remembered something Daniel had said—that the Elite Awards weren't just about glitz and applause. They were about business. About building relationships and connecting with people you normally wouldn't have access to. It dawned on me—I was living that moment. Somehow, despite the drama of shoving Tanya and spilling wine on people, I was still reaping fruit just by being present with Daniel that night.

I continued with the ladies' present. I stood back enough to speak to the small crowd before me. "Thank you all for your kind words and gestures. I'm so incredibly grateful that you took time out of your morning to come see me—and for choosing me as your event specialist. Whether it was the Golden Reader article, the Elite Awards, or something else that brought you here—it doesn't matter. You're here, and for that, I'm truly thankful." I smiled into the group, feeling for a moment like I was on a campaign trail.

"I'd love to talk with each of you individually to get a feel for your heart and vision, so I can help make your event not just beautiful—but yours. Because your event," I said, with a slight dramatic pause, "will be... *you*."

They smiled and nodded, visibly moved by my words. My signature line had landed.

"This is usually our creative hour," I added. "My other appointments don't start until one o'clock. So, I'll take the first person who arrived, and the rest of you are welcome to schedule appointments at your convenience."

Then, a strong accent entered the atmosphere. "I'm your first appointment for today then." Then the body that belonged to that hand arose.

Oh no... why?

It was Dr. Demitri Sokolov. The aggressive Russian from the Elite Awards.

I looked back at April to see if this was true. She nodded—but she quickly caught the confusion in my face.

"Do you want me to...?" she whispered.

I whispered back, "It's okay, April. I'll take him."

I pushed out a smile, even though my insides felt unsure.

"Demitri—hello again. How can I help you today?"

"Well," he said, straightening his blazer, "I'm planning a dinner for the Board of Directors at my club. I was hoping you could assist."

"Sure," I replied. "Give me a couple of minutes to get ready and we'll get started."

I walked into my office, tidied up quickly, and opened the floor-length blinds to let in the natural light. A couple of minutes later, I stepped back out and opened the door.

"Demitri, please—come in."

He entered with a subtle, crooked smile. I closed the door behind him.

For a while, he said nothing. He paced the room slowly. His eyes roamed. Then he spoke.

"Wow," he finally said. "So spacious. So chic."

I could tell he was studying me—trying to read me through my space, just as I often read clients to understand their vision. So, I cut to the chase.

"Demitri—why are you here? Really?"

He turned with faux innocence. "What do you mean?"

"What is this really about?"

"I was intrigued by you last week," he said casually. "Your wit. Your beauty. Your art. You seemed like someone I could talk to... about Mr. Influential," he added, gesturing toward the wall of photos showcasing my events.

I narrowed my eyes. "If this is just some petty attempt to get back at Daniel because of Tanya—don't waste your time. It's elementary and petty, and I don't have time for either."

He chuckled. "No... no. I must say, that would be tantalizing... but no. You really did intrigue me last week. And knowing Daniel—and his soft spot for women—I had to come talk to *you*."

I crossed my arms. He continued.

"See, Daniel is standing in the way of one of the biggest deals of the decade. I'm a major contributor... and I stand to gain a lot. But he doesn't see the beauty in it—the change it could bring to the world."

"Okay…" I said cautiously. ""And what is my role in all of this? I hope you don't think I will persuade or convince him of any agenda of yours—and really, I don't even know you."

He leaned in slightly. "Well… I think you must."

I stared at him—stunned.

I gasped. *Is this guy serious?* At that moment I wanted to tell Demitri to get out, but curiosity was keeping him, and both he and I knew it.

"What deal are you talking about—and why is it so important?"

Demitri didn't answer. Instead, his voice dipped into something else entirely.

"I can see why Daniel's crazy about you," he said. "You're beautiful, strong, independent, and intelligent—I find that incredibly irresistible."

He had just pivoted the whole conversation. I ignored the compliment and waited. Now *I* was studying *him*. Demitri's eyes were fixed on a photo of Daniel and me that sat quietly on the sun-filled wall.

"You know, right?" he asked, his voice rising slightly.

"Know what?" I responded, irritation beginning to coil inside me.

"Why Tanya and I aren't together. I'm sure the gentlemen the other night shared a few tales."

"I heard Daniel took her away."

"Something like that," he admitted. "But I sort of pushed her… so I don't blame her completely. I certainly thought she was stronger—I must admit."

I looked at him with clear confusion etched in my face.

"This deal I am working on is going to revolutionize the world. A plan so beautiful it can change everything we do in the world for the better. But Charles's software is the key."

Okay…he sort of changed the subject again…

"And Daniel…Daniel… got to Charles before one of us," he said with a shrewd undertone.

Us? I thought. Demitri answered my thoughts.

"Some of them you may know. Marco Umbuntu. The rising star from the other night, and others you need not worry yourself about."

"You mean the guy who won the rising star award, right?"

"Yes," he said with an extra smile as if he was name-dropping to somehow seduce me into buying what he was selling. Demitri continued.

"We were after Charles Appleton's software. It provides the ability for another invention, and the other invention will blow this world away—but, no, no, no, we have a closed door due to this... Daniel, this Professor Pacini." Demitri shook his head and continued.

"Because of his influence on Charles—Charles so happens to listen to everything he says—I wonder sometimes—how is that?"

"Favor," I replied, simply.

Demitri's jaw flexed. "Well... that so-called favor needs to be shot down."

"You can't close a door God opens—or open a door God shuts."

Demitri looked at me with aggravated eyes, his demeanor tattled that he was filled with indignation—it seemed me mentioning God irritated his very being.

Demitri continued.

"Is everything religion with you and Daniel? Can't you two come into the real world? Religion is a man-made thing, Ms. Opal."

"Well first, religion is not everything to us...but God is...there is nothing made up about Him. He is everywhere and in everything. God is more real than both of us."

"Is that right, princess? Then where is He? And don't give me that wind argument."

"Wind argument?"

"You can't see the wind, but you know it exists because you can feel and hear it."

"No, that's not where I was going—but hey, that's good!"

"Please...you Christians and your imaginations..." he mocked.

"Hey, that's good...let's talk about that then—what is imagination?"

Demitri looked like I surprised him. I continued.

"Is it something you can tangibly feel—this imagination? Is it something you can grab and hug? No. But it's alive and moving, because it shows up in created things, which proves its existence.

Before a man created the car the idea started in his imagination. I can't see his thoughts, his dreams, and/ or creativity of heart—but it shows up in the thing he created. Imagination is very much a spiritual thing—you can't see it, manipulate it, or touch it physically, but it is powerfully evident through the physical. Imagination is just a peek into the understanding of the spiritual world.

God is Spirit. So, we can start there, Demitri—It is the unseen that creates the things that are seen. God is more real than you and I."

Demitri shouted, "I'm god! I'm god of my own life—I make the rules!" He loosened his necktie and composed his suit jacket.

"Back to the reason for me being here," he belted.

I just stood back, a spectator to this guy's madness.

"Daniel convinced Charles not to go ahead with this deal with us because it allowed huge gaps for illegal activity. Charles bought into it."

Demitri chuckled, this time with a slight anger behind his voice. "This decision literally will cost us a quarter of a billion dollars."

I responded. "I don't understand, Demitri. Because of Daniel's input, the trajectory of Charles' company is headed for a half a billion within the next couple of years, so why would he be pressed to enter something Daniel is telling him otherwise not to do?"

Demitri snapped again. "Because it's the type of money and opportunity you just don't pass up—and it is meddling with my current affairs."

He looked at me then, catching the rising frustration on my face. His tone softened slightly.

"Charles thinks the world of Daniel. I just want him—and others—to see that Daniel is just a man. Not, as you Christians say... a prophet."

"Daniel *is* just a man, Demitri. But God can use whomever He pleases. And when He does... it's wise to listen."

"It's wise to be the captain of your own ship, Ms. Cleverson."

"Sure," I said. "But can you control the waves? Or the wind? Because if they rise with enough force, they can overturn any ship—at any time."

I could tell my answers were frustrating him. His face twitched ever so slightly, as if I was ruining whatever narrative he had already built about me.

Then he continued.

"I wanted to expose Daniel—to Charles, to the others. I wanted to prove that this God of his isn't real. That he isn't some prophet—I debated him often, and sent all types of things his way, but..."

Demitri chuckled creepily.

"Nothing moved him, to my surprise—so eventually I sent my Tanya."

I know he did not just say he used Tanya as a Delilah...

Ooh... I wanted him out of my presence so badly—but my curiosity vastly exceeded my desire. *Patience, Opal... patience,* I told myself. A second later, another thought pushed forward: *This dude is crazy.* I felt Angel's voice rubbing up against my conscience.

"She was sent in to seduce Daniel," Demitri said flatly. "And she did."

He looked me dead in my eyes, searching for a reaction. But I didn't budge. I had him figured out now—but I needed more. I wanted the full story.

"She was supposed to change his mind," he went on. "And he was falling apart. But then—one day—he ended it. To my surprise. And when he did, Tanya had this so-called epiphany that she loved him—what a load of crap, his voice spiked."

"And why didn't you see that coming?" I asked, raising a brow with a slight chuckle. "You've met Daniel. He's not just attractive—he's magnetic. Women want to be with him, and men want to be him."

"Yes... but Tanya is influential too." He stared at me without blinking.

"I'm sorry," I said, pausing. "But why would you *send* your own partner to another man?" I cocked my head. "Especially a man like Daniel? Make it make sense."

"She was just sent in to get intel. Woo him. Study him. Find what makes him tick. She's a master at that. But instead of her getting into him... he impressed onto her. I was disappointed."

Demitri shook his head.

"Well, first of all," I said, "you clearly don't know Daniel. He would *never* be with another man's woman."

"He didn't know we were still together, princess," he replied.

I stared at him for a moment—stunned not just by his words, but by the fact that he was even sharing all this with me. Then suddenly... it clicked.

"Now it all makes sense." I said.

"What exactly?" he asked.

"You witnessed his reactions with Tanya—and researched his history with women and concluded that you know the one thing that can get to Daniel—a woman. So, you are here not so much to get me to comply with your plan, because you know I would never do that. You're here to *read me*. Because you know—if you can get to me, you might just get to Daniel."

I narrowed my eyes. "Daniel's always been the target. He's a threat to your entire worldview—your gods of power, money, and your illusion of control."

Demitri grunted and his stare became cold. I continued.

"It angers you, doesn't it, that you can't influence him with your false gods—that you can't touch him?"

As I said that, the lines in Demitri's face created this angry image before me. I felt the hate seeping out of those lines. He leaned in farther.

"Are you trying to lecture me?"

I remained quiet. But I kept looking at him dead in his eyes.

He snatched my wrist in a horrible grip.

"Young lady, you do not know who you are dealing with or what you are dealing with. Daniel needs to convince Charles to get on board—and most of all, Daniel needs to stop snooping into my current affairs or he is dead—no more gentlemen gestures."

I tried to snatch my arm away, but his grip was powerful it pulled my whole body in."

"Get off me!"

Demitri kept staring at me as his clutch sank deeper. But I would not cower down—I stared at him back. He smirked slightly, then removed his grip and tidied his suit jacket.

I ran to the door.

"Get Out!"

"This never happened."

"Oh, yes it did!"

"Trust me, if you value Daniel's life, and yours—this never happened."

As I swung the door open I felt warm tears falling down my cheeks. I was so angry.

"Don't you ever come back!"

When I opened the door Demitri's face dropped. I looked up when I recognized that woodsy smell I love so much. It was…It was… Daniel….

"I thought I heard a loud shout," Daniel said, eyes scanning first my face, then Demitri's. His expression shifted instantly—from concern to fury.

He saw my tears.

In one hand he held my favorite lilacs—soft, purple, and full of meaning. The other hand began to ball into a fist. His knuckles turned white.

Demitri's face remained cold, and that coldness only fanned the flames. Daniel's rage ignited.

In a flash, he lunged and shoved Demitri. The force sent the man flying several feet back into my office. Daniel slammed my office door behind him and started moving towards Demitri with an intimidating force. He was pink, and veins popped out of his neck.

Demitri got up quickly, looking incrementally afraid the closer Daniel got. That cold stare was gone. Fear was present now. Demitri moved back, almost tripping. Daniel closed the distance between them and raised his hand, which I knew as gentle, and balled it up and rushed it clean across Demitri's face.

I was shocked. That was not the cool and collected Daniel I knew. Nope, it sure was not. Vengeance had been smeared all across

Demitri's face. Demitri was already on Daniel's hot button list, but when he harmed me, he awakened a sleeping giant.

Demitri flinched back from the forceful blow and fell to the ground. His fall was awkward, his limbs were all over the place after being dazed from that punch. It looked like his body was trying to find balance. He shook his head slightly, then looked at Daniel with shocked eyes. I guess he thought he could emotionally bully Daniel, but that bully just received an awakening.

Demitri quickly lifted himself up in a sloppy manner and ran towards the door belting out, "I know what hurts you."

Daniel did not like what his comment meant—possible harm to me, to get to him. Daniel started walking towards Demitri again—briskly. I knew I had to do something, he was out of his common sense, out of his composure—out of him. I jumped right in front of him, hoping I could appease the lion. I grabbed Daniel's face in hopes of calming him, to hush the fire before me. But he sort of moved me to the side. He was focused—and hot. I ran back in front of him and shut the door behind Demitri.

"Daniel, please, please calm down." I spoke in gentle and hushed tones. "He truly is not worth it."

"Calm Daniel, calm…. I'm right here…."

I stroked his hair slowly. It seemed time slowed down a bit, a pause manifested. Then I looked into the galaxy of his eyes and, as I focused on them, his enlarged eyes slowly lowered. Oddly, my attempt to comfort and hush him, comforted me. The sudden moment drew me in and his eyes pulled on every fiber of my heart. They were beautiful, as always, however, they were vulnerable, and something was missing in them. I wanted to fill in that missing something—that gap, that lack that stared back at me and left me feeling its emptiness. My eyes grazed his strong face to let him know everything was ok.

Oh, how I missed this man, I thought.

Daniel slowly and carefully reached out and stroked the side of my face. I responded by pressing my head into his strong hand.

"What did he do?"

"He tried to threaten me—He grabbed me by my wrist."

Daniel looked up in the air and bit his lips.

"He is going to pay for this, Opal."

"No, No… vengeance is the Lord's."

"But I should have protected you."

"You did Daniel—you did."

I stroked his face again with my hands. Daniel looked at my lips and then I looked at his. I felt him exhale. Then I exhaled.

In that moment I knew, without any words spent, that all was forgiven. The yearning was real and evident. I could almost hear panting in my spirit among us, like a whining pant a pooch has for his human when they are leaving, or when the dog is wounded. Our distance from each other had hurt both of us. I thought it was just me.

Our proximity, our yearning, elicited a passion that dripped out of our bodies. Our lips rushed together and pressed in—they screamed out for touch. Our breaths became heavy. It was like a part of each of us was broken without the other and the heat we felt was melting us to coagulate back together.

The union shouted out of our eyes and manifested through the unrestrained impulses of our hands. Quickly, the embrace elevated. I could feel my heart racing between the aggressive kisses—then suddenly, Daniel threw down his hands and turned around and screamed. He had to let it out. The beast. He knew he had to contain it. It was getting way more heated than usual—too fast, and it seemed that scream alerted both of us to wake up, wake up from the creeping desire that was consuming us in the moment. We had completely forgotten where we were, and we had to remember our oath. In only seconds, we'd been completely lost in each other. I felt very awkward, heated, wanting Daniel like never before. But I also knew I couldn't do anything with that yet. Just looking at the sweat softly resting on him did something to me. I composed myself and looked at Daniel. He returned a hot desire look and we knew we needed to cool down fast.

"Opal, wait right there please—I'm going to the restroom.'"

"Well… I need to go too," I said.

We looked at each other and understood. We both went to the restroom.

I'd been in the bathroom a couple of minutes and was patting away the water I'd splashed on my face when I received a text: It's been thirty minutes. Are you able to see another person?

I texted April back: *Yes, just give me 5 minutes please, and you can send the next person into my office.* I'd almost forgotten about all the people who came in this morning to see me. I was in a whirlwind, one thing after another. In addition to that, it seemed my life was turning into this emotional showroom. And I had so many questions for Daniel, starting with Tanya and this crazy, demented, Demitri character. I took a couple of deep breaths while fixing my shuffled clothing, then came out the restroom.

Daniel was waiting with open arms. I ran into them.

"I thought I lost you," he said.

I hugged him tightly and lifted my head to look up at his tall frame draped over me. I looked into his eyes again. "No, you haven't," I responded.

He kissed me gently on my lips.

"But I think we have to continue after work," I said.

"I think you're right," he chuckled.

"Until later then?" he asked, focusing on my face.

"Later," I responded.

"Six or seven?"

I looked around.

"I believe seven."

He kissed me again. Once on the lips. Once on my forehead. Then softly on my hand.

"I love you, Opal."

"I love you."

And then he walked away.

In full euphoria, I peeked back at him. Euphoria mixed with a little pain as the physical distance between us grew. It pinched my heart. I looked ahead, then back at him again. Suddenly Daniel raised his arms in the air like Rocky Balboa after a victory. I laughed joyfully and then headed back to the lobby for my next guest.

CHAPTER 8

I walked out of my office to greet my last appointment—whew, what a day. I wanted this one to go by swiftly. I wanted to be in united bliss with my Daniel. As I walked out, I noticed that the last appointment was with a man who had familiar features. He stood and extended his rather large hand to me. I looked at that hand and remembered the burn scar that lived there. That burn happened from a failed experiment I was a spectator of. I looked up at his extra smile.

Oh, how could I ever... have forgotten, Aric?

"Aric!"

"Opal!" he belted back.

Aric opened his arms wide, and we hugged.

"Wow—Aric Singleton!"

I swiftly looked at April.

"April, this is Aric Singleton."

April looked a little confused.

"I told you about him some time ago—my first crush."

"Ohhh…" she sighed with a trying smile. April was trying her best to make sense of my crazy day. I could tell she was really pushing that smile.

I turned back to Aric. I could not believe the day I was having; if I told anyone about it, they wouldn't believe me. I guess I was getting tested or something—and he had the nerve to be my last appointment? He looked handsome. Those cute features had developed into strong chin lines and hardened cheekbones. He had long, shoulder-length hair that looked like he'd just left the salon. He was a little heavier than I remembered, particularly in the gut, but still very handsome.

"How are you—what brings you here?" I belted.

"I saw your picture on the Golden Reader, and I said—I know her—I grew up with her. I have to see her!" Aric said enthusiastically.

"It's me...." I responded and stretched open my arms.

"And look at you—you became such a beautiful woman," he said.

"Aw, stop it."

"You did—I had to come see you myself."

"All well. How are things with you?" I changed the subject. I felt a bit uneasy accepting that flattery and loving it—especially just hours after embracing my Daniel.

"Good." He stated.

"Well, that's awesome. Please, come into my office."

I beckoned him in and looked back at April with enlarged eyes and raised arms. She looked at me with concern while shaking her head. It was as if I could hear her thoughts—talking about my crazy, unpredictable, rollercoaster of a day, indeed it was. The people. Tanya. Demitri. Daniel... and now Aric. Aric was my first childhood love and a former best friend. He taught me a lot as a youth, including how to swim, how to climb, and how to ride rough terrain on my bike, which left scars that I still have to this day. We were friends from the tender age of four to fourteen.

I sat down on the lounge sofa with Aric in my office.

"Wow, Opal, you really did well for yourself," Aric stated, his eyes scanning my office.

"All...thanks," I said and shrugged my shoulders. "How is your family?" I said swiftly. "Good—thanks," Aric responded.

"And what are you doing with yourself, sir?"

"I'm an engineer."

"I'm not surprised, you were always trying to solve a problem by making little stuff."

"Oh, you remember that?"

"How can I not, that sort of stuff left that burn on your hand."

"Yeah, my experiment with that corn oil." "Yeah—you were always experimenting." We both laughed.

"Well, how long has it been?" he asked.

"Technically, we stopped being friends when I was about fourteen, but the last time I saw you was at age twenty-five, and you were tied up with your family at the Opera. Do you remember?"

"Yes, sorry about that, Opal. I meant to reach out, but we were in the middle of the show. At the end, I looked for you—but, hold up, let's rewind here. You said we stopped being friends when you were fourteen. What do you mean?"

"Aric, seriously, come on now."

"What?"

"Do you remember Lake Truth or Dare?"

"Yes… of course."

"Well…our relationship sort of dwindled from there."

Aric wore a look of complete confusion on his face. Around age thirteen, Aric started taking me to a lake we called Lake Truth or Dare. Lake Truth or Dare was a secluded spot, enclosed by large and small rocks, with a narrow opening that served as a trail leading back to a vast lake with a breathtaking horizon. We used the big rocks as chairs and jumped the small, smooth rocks across the water to create ripple effects. It was a place the kids in the neighborhood went to play, to get their first kiss, camp, and share secrets. Many stupid, goofy, and crazy dares were made and carried out at Lake Truth or Dare.

He was sixteen and I was thirteen the first time he brought me there. I remember he would take me up to this lake just to feel me all over. He was doing things to me that he certainly should not have been doing to me at that age. He introduced me to sensory experiences I had not known were there. I allowed myself to be open to discovery, not really knowing what I was allowing.

I only allowed Aric, whelp, because he was Aric. Aric was older than the other boys, tougher, smarter, and funny, and he taught me everything. Because of those reasons—I loved Aric. However, with him, I soon found a worldly reality at Lake Truth or Dare: the power of the physical and its hold on people.

One day, I went to the lake with Aric and another friend of mine, Adalee. Adalee was a beautiful, fun, and bold girl. Everyone liked being around Adalee. She was like the big sister in the neighborhood; all the girls my age and younger looked up to her. She was like a young Wonder Woman with her daredevil self. She was tall and filled in for her age—and tough. She could have been thought of as seventeen or maybe eighteen when she was only turning fifteen.

That day at the lake, a truth or dare was called. Adalee chose the dare, as usual. Aric asked Adalee to do something that shocked me. He asked her to do something that I knew my grandma would classify as nasty. He dared Adalee to take off her shirt. Without a second thought—she did it. Then he dared her to take off her bra. She did it swiftly. Again, without any thought.

When she did, Aric's eyeballs got as wide as saucers. I believe my eyes did as well. I could not believe how developed she was. Then I looked at my chest, which was just that—a chest, flat, like a board. I then looked back at Adalee and then at Aric. His fixation on her was overwhelming to me. Then I instantly felt something I'd never felt before, a non-desirable feeling, a twinge of wanting what someone else had, and not liking them for it: jealousy.

She had something I didn't have, and he wanted her for it. After that moment, I felt uneasy. I felt something moving in a direction I could not control. I felt his curiosity for me retracting, pulling away with every second, and it was being poured into Adalee. So that evening, when the lights warned us it was time to go home, Aric did not kiss me. He did not give me the thing I loved the most that we had started putting into practice. Instead, he hugged me. That action solidified the reversal of our relationship.

After that day, Aric never came to pick me up again. Lake Truth or Dare was something I had heard about through other teenagers' stories, but one I would never live through again. I heard he was always taking Adalee there, and after six months with no response from him, I heard they were dating. When I turned fourteen, I just knew Aric would come see me, because he always showed up for my birthday—but this time he did not. It was like he moved away—but he hadn't. He was just two blocks away.

Shortly after, I heard Aric was taking Adalee to the dance. It was my first dance, and I always wanted Aric to take me. When he never called—and was never around when I went to his house, I knew he had totally forgotten about me. It was as if this girl bewitched him. I wanted that type of attention—love—why did she have it—and not me?

The sequence of events nearly killed me, but it taught me a valuable lesson. It taught me I was not pretty enough to keep his love—that I wasn't enough. My inadequacy left tears that saturated my pillowcase at night. I cried and cried because this reminded me of my biological father in a way. My biological father left me and my mother for another woman—a much younger woman.

I hated that feeling of rejection. I started to hate the way I looked—the way I was built. That experience taught me that I needed to look a certain way to be loved. It was the birthing ground of my physical insecurity. And even when I obtained my curves years later, I always found myself comparing myself to other women. It took me until my late twenties to find and fully embrace my own unique beauty.

Now, back to that present time and out of the memory bank, it dawned on me why Aric was here. I believe Aric's presence here, on this day, was to reveal to me where my root insecurity came from, and although I was sure now of who I was and of my God-given beauty, that insecurity was still lingering like a nagging fly. It came spiraling back with Daniel. I never really killed the lie. The lie that I am not good enough to be loved. To be loved by the one I loved.

It was such a poignant, illegitimate lesson to learn in relation to my first heartbreak; a perspective molded into my belief system in one inexperienced moment. When my father left my mother and me, I thought it was just my father who couldn't love me—but when Aric left me for Adalee, the perspective became sealed, and now it included all males. I also realized at some point that I had become what I hated about my biological father—I became vain—and externally driven.

I began to look for the most attractive, and I also wanted to be the most attractive, but of course, time disappointed. With guys, I realized that the best-looking, dreamy boys were always empty and self-focused—no real substance. They only dished out pain by the droves. And I realized that there was always someone more beautiful than myself.

My thoughts jumped off Aric and my father onto Daniel. How could I keep forgetting…? I kept forgetting what God revealed early on with Daniel. I was forgetting through the shadow of my past. I let past circumstances blind me, scare me back into that fearful corner—into a room I was left in, alone.

I closed my eyes and offered a silent prayer of thanks to Jesus in my heart. As I did this, Aric cleared his throat.

"Are you okay?"

"Sorry, I just received a revelation—something huge," I said to Aric.

"What is that?" Aric stated.

"I'll share, but I didn't know if you were finished."

"Well...ok…" Aric stated.

"What do you mean I stop talking to you, you stopped talking to me."

"No, sir, as I remember, your nasty behind was groping me in places you shouldn't have been at all at that age—I didn't know any better. Unfortunately, I was your experiment at that time. And when Adalee came around with her newly developed self—you forgot all about me."

Aric gave me a silent stare. His face grew somewhat uneasy.

"Yeah, I was wrong. I did not have any business doing that—but I was young, too. I am not justifying my actions or anything; I'm just saying that there is a part of me that didn't know any better either. I didn't know how to handle those hormones."

When Aric said that, my heart knew, right there, what I needed to do.

"And that's why I closed my eyes momentarily there Aric—I was thanking God. See, I had to be reminded where my deep insecurity came from, and I had to forgive you, my father—and others for embedding it."

"Wow...well, ok..." Aric looked subtly stunned.

"Sorry to put a damper on our reunion. I went deep and dramatic pretty fast," I said with a slight chuckle.

"No need to be sorry. I'm sorry, Opal."

"All is forgiven. It's old news now, and like you said, we both were very young at that time—but I do hope that you are better now at handling yourself."

"Oh, believe me, I think I learned. I have four daughters."

I stretched my eyes.

"Oool...you're going to get it...." I replied.

"I'm already getting it."

I chuckled a bit, and Aric joined me.

"I'm surprised these moments caused deep issues," Aric said while lightly putting his hand over mine.

"Well, Aric, I'm realizing a lot of the issues we have in life as adults were birthed in our youth—and it wasn't just you—it started with my father, but it was sealed with you—others sort of buried those issues within as well."

"Wow, woman, you became deep within," Aric responded. We both chuckled.

Then, for a singular moment, I received another revelation. I was reminded of that young girl at Young Cry who exposed herself—she exposed herself like Adalee. It took me back to a wound that was still so open. It was a smelly wound that was manifesting itself through presumptuous decisions and rampant paranoia.

I thought Tanya triggered the night—but that wasn't really the case. It was that young girl—she was a reminder that maybe my love would leave me for someone better, more beautiful, younger. Tanya was just the gasoline added to an already kindled fire. Oh, how the enemy was reveling in that moment. He wanted to tap dance on my fear of rejection, which was instilled in me by my father and Aric years ago.

As the hour passed by, Aric shared his problems with boys trying to prey on his girls now. He shared it in such a comical way however, he had me cracking up. I forgot how funny he was. And the more I laughed with Aric, the more my soul was mending.

Later, inside Daniel's car, I said, "Daniel, why does this Demitri want to harm you—What are you into with him?" Daniel cleared his throat.

"Heath and I found that Demitri is behind some very disturbing things—I don't want to speak on it fully because we don't have enough information yet regarding his involvement—but we have information on his colleague Marco, for sure.

"What information?"

"Possible trafficking—and more."

"Hold up, human trafficking?"

"Yes, Opal," Daniel said with frowning eyes. A new, sophisticated way of trafficking that is monstrous.

My stomach turned.

"It seems, however, that Demitri's routes regarding his cigar empire are for more than cigars—it may be some sort of cover. Heath and I believe Demitri and Marco were trying to use Charles's software to accelerate their communications, transportation, and the discretion of their products and/or goods—which we are discovering may not be goods at all—but people—people sold and abused at astronomical amounts through a system."

"I was only able to find this out because Charles asked me what I thought about him linking up with Marco and Demitri, so to provide an answer, I did some research. In researching, I found some very disturbing things, which forced me to go down a terribly shocking rabbit whole of dark discovery. I asked Heath to join me to look into some things—he did and found more information about Marco that can be incriminating—but there are missing pieces where Demitri is involved—but shades of his involvement keeps appearing."

I shook my head in astonishment. It was so hard to believe men so accomplished could be so involved in such a thing.

"I don't understand, Daniel—these men are teachers—leaders, they have a higher learning—they should know better."

"Well, Opal, education can be dangerous sometimes with the wrong heart. If a person is a thief in their heart, if you educate them, they will just become a bigger thief. What is in one's heart is how one may move. Education and/or information will provide them the means to do what's in their heart on a larger scale."

Daniel cleared his throat a little more. Then added, "Speaking of the heart—we have more serious things to talk about."

"And what is more serious than that man threatening you—us?"

"Our relationship—us—what's going on between us—we have to talk about it."

"Yes, I know..."

Daniel started pushing out his words forcibly. He was backed up.

"Opal, do you honestly believe there is any relationship that doesn't have its trials?"

"No, of course not," I responded.

"Well, this was one of ours... You said I was the perfect guy for you, so why did you run away that night so easily?"

"I..." Daniel cut me off and kept spilling out.

"You are the perfect woman for me—that's why I am here—I will fight to have you with me, but I have to know if you are willing to fight to have me with you?"

He grabbed my hands, "I love Opal—you. Yes, there are beautiful women—there are beautiful women everywhere. I cannot help that! And I might even be pursued, just like you may be pursued, but you must have faith that I'm not looking to pursue any woman back!" Daniel grunted slightly.

"Is Tanya beautiful? Yes. Do I want her—no! Don't let your fears put a sock in my mouth."

"What...?" I responded.

"I told you what broke Tanya and me up, if it were just mere beauty I was looking for, I would be with her. My body wanted her, but our spirits were at war—I told you that. You and I are different. We spend hours talking and meditating on things—I can't share that with anyone else—I told you that!" Daniel said. "But the moment an incident occurs regarding a woman, it's like you forget everything... Like you forget who I am."

His eyes became more intense.

"My soul wants you—Opal. I can minister with you in ways I cannot find anywhere else—that is what makes you a unique beauty—it's your soul mirrored to mine. But you are drowning me out by not listening to my words, by stuffing my mouth with a liar sock—you do not trust me."

I let Daniel speak; I needed to let Daniel vent—I snatched that away from him with unanswered calls and texts. I think he got it all out, for he stared at me silent, waiting for my reply. I waited for a second longer to make sure.

Pause.

I responded.

"No... It is not so much that I don't trust you, Daniel. It was me. I believed deep down that I was not good enough for you—that maybe you would leave me because I was not good enough for you, and... my lack of faith in myself made me have a lack of faith in you."

Tears gushed out of my eyes as I said those words. I exposed myself. I was already too open and tender from earlier, but those words that slipped out pressed a slight embarrassment in my chest to say this out loud. I lowered my head slightly.

"Are you serious?" Daniel chuckled.

"You're the gift, Opal."

He put his strong hand, which was glued to mine, onto the pit of his chest.

"Opal—look at me." I slowly looked at him.

"O.... how can I ever leave you if I believe God chose you for me—gave you to me—how can I ever leave that?"

Daniel looked at me with eyes filled with resolve.

"You're my wife."

I looked closer at Daniel as he declared a title I did not own yet.

"I really knew when we were baptized at the Jordan River. I never told you, but there was this aura around you. Not so much like a light, but a presence wrapped in a light that I felt every time you entered a room and/or space I was in—I knew God was telling me then, there was something about you."

I chuckled.

"What's so funny?" Daniel responded.

"Because that's when I started seeing you differently. Why didn't you tell me?"

"I wanted to tell you the night before our wedding. I wanted it to be a special moment when I shared that—but now, I believe the time is fitting."

I smiled. "Look at God."

I shook my head, and I wanted to tell Daniel about Aric and how my healing process really started two hours ago, but I felt it wasn't the time, especially at this vulnerable moment. I felt bringing up another individual, especially a past boyfriend, would dilute the moment of intimacy we were in. I just listened.

Daniel spoke while stroking my hair.

"People are beautiful, Opal—God makes beautiful things, but you must know, you are one of them. You are my desire inside and out, the promise I have been waiting for, and I will fight to honor that, not dishonor that. But you must know and have faith in this relationship and wear it as a badge for the world to see."

Daniel squinted at me with intense eyes. "I rebuke this strong-hold of insecurity in Yeshua's name—God loves you—I love you!" Daniel belted.

Daniel then kissed me on my head, his lips, warm. That kiss felt like it produced a healing anointing oil that seeped inside my skin and into my mind. Daniel started praying over me. As he spoke, his words penetrated and hit something, that lost door my sisters took me to the other day in prayer, and Aric opened two hours ago. I realized God was using Daniel to pull out what was hidden behind it—that lingering thing.

I looked at him and I realized that with us, there were no more walls. They had shattered into sheer dust. Vulnerability was our very essence at that moment, and when he stared at me, that stare went straight into my being—he was looking for something, that lingering something.

Then he found the open door. He found the open door with the intenseness of his eyes. Those eyes found her—a part of me—that lingering thing was a part of me. A confused, insecure fourteen-year-old little girl. As he caressed my face with his hands, he slowly brought her out. I felt every authentic chord from his body resonate off him and seep into my veins. His eyes, still, so serious. I could see the frustration and pain that temporarily lived there. The moment, raw, open, and exposed. As he continued to pray, I felt every bit of his words, like they plucked my every nerve. Staring into his eyes, I started to tear up even more. I felt guilty for his suffering, for our suffering for these past weeks—it was so unnecessary. I realized that undealt with things brought about unnecessary situations.

His love hovered over me, descending on me like a thin layer of early morning dew. It overwhelmed every part of my body, so much so, that I trembled as the liquid salt covered my lips. It looked like joy entered his eyes. Then that joy awakened that shallow dimple.

Daniel stopped praying and said to me,

"If I were Jacob, you would be my Rachel. I would work years for you. If I were Solomon, you would be my Shulamite. Out of all those women he had at his disposal, it was one—the Shulamite woman you hear of his intoxicating love for, not his seven hundred wives and three hundred concubines—that must have been some woman," he said in a joking way, kissing me on my forehead again. But I want no other woman, I just want one—you know that O."

Daniel started to recite the Song of Solomon:

"Like a lily among thorns, so is my love among the daughters."

Daniel kissed my left cheek, then continued.

"I have compared you, my love, my filly among Pharaoh's chariots. Your cheeks are lovely with ornaments, your neck with chains of gold."

Daniel then kissed my right cheek and then the center of my neck. I joined in with Daniel, sharing in the verses.

"Behold, you are handsome, my beloved! Yes, pleasant!"

I kissed him on his forehead and then slowly down to his beard, which I felt grazing my face. I inhaled, loving his smell. Then, I looked at him with assuring eyes, then continued.

"I am dark, but lovely, O daughters of Jerusalem, like the tents of Kedar, like the curtains of Solomon."

Daniel interceded, "You're dark and lovely Opal, no buts."

"No butts?"

We both chuckled.

"You know what I mean." Daniel smiled.

With a second quick breath, he spoke, deepening his voice.

"You have dove's eyes behind your veil. Your hair is like a flock of goats, going down from Mount Gilead.

As Daniel said that, he wove his hands through my curly mane and then continued.

"Your teeth are like a flock of shorn sheep which have come up from the washing, every one of which bears twins and none is barren among them. Your lips are like a strand of scarlet, and your mouth is lovely. Your temples behind your veil are like a piece of pomegranate. Your neck is like the tower of David, built for an armory, on which hang a thousand bucklers, all shields of mighty men.

And although your external beauty captivates me, O—it is your spirit that captivates me much more."

I grabbed Daniel by the collar of his shirt and yanked him to me. We kissed. Passionately.

CHAPTER 9

anya had deep purple and red bruises smeared across her right eye, stretching to the temples of her head. That rich, bronze tan from a couple of weeks ago was gone. The park where we were meeting was lonely this morning. There was the pond, the bench, and the occasional jogger—and of course, Tanya, Daniel, and me—thank goodness.

"I thought it was supposed to be you and I, Opal?" Tanya blurted, while looking at Daniel and our clutched hands.

"The information was for me—right?" Daniel snapped.

"Yes, but…"

"But what, Tanya? Is this some sick game? My heart belongs to Opal. That is it."

Tanya started weeping, then snapped back, "It's no game—I just didn't want you to see me like this!"

She was embarrassed. Looking at her face, I knew immediately who the culprit was. I spoke.

"Did Demitri do this to you?"

She looked at me as if she were surprised, I knew who hit her. She looked at Daniel and then back at me, nodding her head. Daniel and I briefly looked at each other.

Daniel hushed his tone. "What's going on, Tanya, and what happened?"

Tanya blurted, "It was me, Daniel, who contacted you and Heath about information on Demitri—I was the one who was supposed to meet up with you that night at the Elite Awards."

Daniel's eyes enlarged. Then he turned towards me to explain. "That's what the late-night gathering was all about at the Elite

Awards—meeting up with this other party sent by Professor Grieves to give us sensitive information on Demitri."

Daniel then turned back to Tanya. "Did Professor Grieves send you—or did you have him call me?"

"I had him call."

"Now, it makes sense."

"What?" Tanya and I said simultaneously.

"The book, the book on my desk—Professor Grieves put it there for you—didn't he? I remember him being in my class the day before it started. Daniel's brows furrowed.

"Yes—but he really didn't look inside."

"How do you know?"

"That man's worldview is exactly like Demitri's—he is not looking into anything that states supernatural."

"He is a professor—he is highly likely to flick through the pages."

"Well—I made sure he didn't open it. Let's keep it like that." Tanya said, waving her hand.

"I'm not even going to ask why he is doing all these irrational things for you," Daniel said.

That comment told me everything. That Tanya had Professor Reives wrapped all around her finger.

Daniel blurted out, "If you had the information—why didn't you just give it to me that night?"

"I still loved you—I still do!"

This woman is awfully honest, I thought.

Daniel clutched my hand. I believe to let me know he was with me.

"I figured I could certainly give to you what you needed to get rid of Demitri," Tanya said, "but I wanted us back—even though I knew maybe you were with someone else. I just didn't know you would be with—her," she said, nodding at me. You could hear the acrimony that lingered.

"Did you know Opal before all of this?"

Daniel looked at Tanya and me.

I shook my head no.

"No—but she is different—that's what I mean," she snapped. Tanya looked directly at me.

"Yeah, I found you and my jealousy, I must admit, consumed me so much, things came out of me I didn't even know were still there. So much so, I left the night bitter and escaped the primary reason I was there."

I responded. "Well, it seems, handing off that information wasn't the primary reason you were there—Daniel was."

Tanya paused briefly. She was staring at me, sort of weird—you could tell her neurons were flying behind that skull of hers. Then she spoke.

"Well...Here you go." Tanya plopped a USB in Daniel's hand.

"I couldn't go straight to the cops—because that man has cops on his payroll—and I don't know who they are."

"You're the only one I trust. Over the past couple of years, I have been researching Demitri and visiting the actual sites of his so-called cigar routes. I knew the only way to be happy with you was to get him out of the way."

"I'm not understanding. We broke up because of our differences."

"No, Demitri told me everything. You left because he threatened you into leaving. I thought I had to stay away until I found out something on him."

"No Tanya…. I'm sorry, I left because we were quite different."

When Tanya heard that, another cast of embarrassment settled over her face, and then she belted out, "He tortured me, you know—before I came to you in the first place, Daniel. I never told you that. He had his men strip me bare, literally in front of his mansion, and he burned all of my things in front of him that he ever gave me—all my clothes, my degrees, my cherished keepsakes. He did this because he wanted to drive home the point that he took me in when I had nothing—that he provided everything for me. But when I started moving for myself, thinking for myself, he did not like it. Then he left me in the snow, literally bare, in front of the gentlemen's club I was working at when I met him."

Tanya reached in her purse to grab a tissue to wipe her running nose. She spoke while she did.

"He told me he'd given me everything and that he, not some higher power, could take it all away." Tanya paused for a breath as she wiped her nose and tears.

"It got to this place because I told him I was leaving him—and that I agreed with a lot of your arguments. I believed in you, Daniel, I believed in us—before there was an us."

"It's too late, Tanya—and it's just not supposed to be."

I started to feel uncomfortable. Although I knew that Daniel was mine and I was his—something felt wrong about being there. I felt like they needed to hash everything out. I knew Daniel had me there to infuse trust, but I felt like I didn't need it anymore. I trusted him, and I trusted that he loved me.

"Maybe, I should go," I said.

"No, he said—I want you here with me."

I looked at Daniel and nodded, and looked at Tanya again—and her face was disappointed.

"How did you get this information?" Daniel belted.

"Well—does it matter? It's there—just know I put myself in harm's way to get it—and it caught up with me, clearly."

"All the phantom accounts I saw were connected to routes all over. They were named after well-known philosophy terms and/or philosophers known for Relativistic ideologies. But I soon recognized that those accounts were the labels of the trafficking routes—human trafficking—Marco and Demitri are involved in."

"Yes, Heath and I know of Marco—we could not find any solidifying information connecting Demitri."

"Well, now you have it—trust me."

As Tanya said that, I remembered when I witnessed that unexpected emotion called jealousy permeate out of Daniel's pores that night with Marco. Now I know it wasn't so much jealousy, but an instinct to protect. Daniel felt like he had to protect me from the threat he knew Marco was.

Tanya continued.

"This information, even anonymously sent, needed care. That's why it had to be you that I give it to! But I promise you what's on here will indict that monster. But you have to give it to whom you need to so that he may go away quickly. My life is on the line now—and so is yours—I guess you have been getting too close."

I looked at Daniel. I remember when Demitri said that to me in the office. He was scared—Daniel must have been close.

Daniel's phone rang.

I'm not going to answer it, he said. He went to hang up, but then glanced at the name. He paused and then said, "No, actually, I have to take this—it's Heath." He glanced at Tanya and then at me, telling us to behave without saying the words.

"I have to take this," he reiterated. He walked away talking, his back to us. Tanya followed him with her eyes, combing over his frame. She threw her head back and combed her fingers through her hair. Then she looked at me and said, "You have something to look forward to—it was the best sex I ever had—and believe I have experience." I scowled slightly and felt a slight heat rise in my chest.

"What is wrong with you?!"

"Jealous." Tanya stated.

"No." "But I feel disrespected—it's like you have no respect for anyone—not even yourself. You lost Daniel because you didn't respect him. You disrespect other people, so they don't even like it when you come into the room—where is your dignity? Why would I be jealous of that?" I snapped.

Tanya gave me a scowling look.

"Do not judge me—you do not know me, and you don't know where I've been in my life."

"I'm not judging—I'm making an analysis. It seems like you believe you can get what you want and do what you want—say what you want, simply because of your looks. Everything is not about looks—sex." "Well, for me, my looks—sex— has been my life, bad or good."

I don't know why, but when she said that, a light bulb went on, and I saw the connections—Demitri met her at a gentlemen's club—she had nothing before him—she stated he pretty much left her naked in the snow at that gentleman's club like he found her—naked. He said he sent Tanya to Daniel to woo him. He said Tanya can be quite influential. And she was able to get inside information on Demitri that no one else could get—she was probably a victim of the sex trade herself.

I looked at Tanya. This time, with concern, her evoking words did not even penetrate me anymore—they couldn't, because now it was in my head that it didn't matter what she said. This issue was no longer about me. Her words showed me, her—her brokenness.

Then I realized, that is the key to "offense". People are so easily offended when we personalize everything. Her actions, her words, revealed her pain—her.

"Tanya, were you—or are you, a victim of the sex trade Demitri's involved in?"

"Victim—what do you mean?" she said, pursing her lips.

"Were you trafficked?"

"Please..." she said, "Do you believe I was subject to people hovering over me enforcing their will over mine? Do you believe that?" she snapped. Tanya's face grew increasingly red.

"I don't believe what you told us, is the only way Demitri is hurting you."

Tanya's red face started creating these wrinkles, which shouted surfacing pain. Sadness. She bit her lip—it looked like she was trying to keep herself from bursting out. Her reaction told me everything.

"Tanya, I'm so sorry..."

When I said that—she broke—tears began to burst out of her eyes, then she ran. Funny thing, she was running away like I was doing a week ago—how quick that table turned. I screamed out for her, "Tanya!"

She kept running.

Daniel, being alerted to my shout, turned around and briskly walked over to me. "What happened?"

"This thing with Demitri and Tanya is bigger than we imagined."

Two days later, it was the bridal rehearsal, a day before the wedding. However, I was in the ladies' room groaning—my spirit twisted. Tanya was certainly on my mind... all of that extra from her was a loud cry for help. I was groaning because the Lord had revealed it to me. In the past, I asked the Lord if he could reveal the spirit of a man first—so I could see his heart, so I would not be seduced by his appearance only—and He blessed me with that with men—then, I found Daniel. However, I came up short-handed—the question should not have stopped with men. I needed to see everyone: male and female.

I ached a bit thinking about Tanya—what she must have gone through—men taking advantage of her for years—and living with Demitri's demented personality—it bothered me. My thoughts rushed to that young girl exposing herself at Young Cry. That young girl thought exposing herself would bring her attention—somehow, some love. Her thinking was so backwards—like many women who have been abused or raised in toxic environments. Toxic acts perpetuated through a perverted perspective—all to reach acceptance, love.

I thought about what happened to me—how it distorted my thinking—where I was healed from the other day. I cried and cried, thinking about everything. I realized that the Lord could not have revealed this to me until that insecure little girl was removed the other day. With her gone, I could now see the other hurting women as well. I could see that jealousy and insecurity could have hurt my witness to other women—other girls, who needed my help. This understanding shows why deliverance is vital!

An hour later, all the ladies and groomsmen were present; however, we were still waiting on Heath and Daniel. Sheila and Purple were my matrons of honor—I could not choose between them. Samantha, Angel, and my cousin Dee Dee were my bridesmaids, and my dear assistant, April, filled in for me today to superintend the wedding rehearsal. The best man was Professor Watts, who was the professor who took Daniel under his wing when he was eighteen.

Professor Watts was a handsome man for his age—a peculiar handsome. His beard was beautiful and rich, a full, healthy-looking beard, perfectly trimmed and white, which he would pull on when he got into one of his intellectual rants. Wisdom imprinted his facial lines. It clothed his face, yet his wrinkles were remarkably soft, barely visible. His body was still erect and strong, which he attributed to daily resistance exercise and walking.

According to Daniel, Professor Watts was a fitness giant in his youth. He was the man who inspired all his debate children to walk into the fitness realm, not just the world of literature and the art of argument. Professor Watts taught him and all his boys the necessity for physical fitness. He believed it improved mental fitness. As a result, it was a mandate to be a part of his team; you had to enter into the world of clean dieting, organic protein shakes, reps, and weights. He was the reason Daniel was so adamant about staying in shape.

I was so glad Professor Watts was there; he made so much of an impression on Daniel. He was more than a mentor to Daniel, he was a father gained to both him and the rest of the guys there. Professor Watts was also going to walk me down the aisle—a gesture Daniel thought would be nice—being I was absent of my biological father.

The groomsmen were some of Daniel's best friends from his debate team. Bobby, Mike, Jordan, and Heath—whom I met not so long ago. I loved looking at our wedding party. It was marvelous. It was like the United Nations. Bobby and Heath were Caucasian, Mike was African American, and Jordan was of Eastern Indian descent. Then you had me and my diverse ladies, and my godchildren—Sheila's children, who were a mix of her Korean and African genes and her husband's Japanese genes—wow, right?

Sheila's twin girls were going to be my flower girls, her boys were going to be my ushers, and her youngest son was going to be my ring bearer. It was fun and interesting to see us together; we were a mod podge of colors filling in a beautiful, framed story.

We joked and intermingled, then a half an hour later, April and I frazzled around waiting for the two we could not continue without. The timing was crucial because everyone had meticulously scheduled lives, and we needed everything to fall into this two-hour slot. Soon, a quarter of an hour passed. I reached for my phone to call Daniel for the fourth time, but before I did, the big, thick church doors opened…and there stood the absent fellas we were all waiting for. Relief and curiosity took hold of me simultaneously. I looked at April across the room and could tell she felt the same. And although I knew April was supposed to take on the worry of this time by ensuring everything was set on schedule, it was hard not to fall into my normal role.

"About time," Professor Watts belted.

"What's the excuse this time—the lady tried to detain you?" Jordan yelled.

"You all be quiet before Watts gets any ideas about putting a sock in my mouth." Daniel responded jokingly. All the guys laughed; it was a hearty laugh from them too—they were clearly enjoying an inside joke. The ladies and I just looked at each other in smiles and subtle dented brows, realizing there was something we were out of the loop about. I did, however, remember that "sock in the mouth" analogy Daniel used not so long ago. I suppose this was something he adopted in his youth with them.

I gazed at Daniel, and he gazed back with shy eyes, almost like a little boy who felt sorry for the act he got caught in. He hurried over to me and we briefly kissed.

"Thanks for making it," I said sarcastically, and poked him.

"Ahh...yeah, Heath and I took care of everything. Demitri and Marco are being apprehended as we speak."

"Praise the Lord," I said, feeling warm tears rise. I thought, Now, Tanya, and probably so many other women will be delivered.

Daniel rubbed my face and started to wipe the tears that hadn't even rolled down my cheeks yet. He kissed me on my cheeks and then hugged me. "It will be ok," he said, "It probably will be a long process—but what Tanya gave me was staggering."

"Good."

I pecked him again and gazed around the room one last time before we started lunch before the rehearsal. My eyes latched onto Angel. She was licking her lips, literally, looking at all the men, especially Heath, who had just entered. They were an attractive bunch—but Angel looked thirsty—too thirsty. I was starting to feel secondhand embarrassment. So, I walked over gracefully and whispered in her ear.

"Angel, you are looking like you want to devour these men, especially Heath—why so obvious?"

"That's what I do to let the man know I'm checking him out."

"Angel, not this type of man. Now, I'm still learning him, but remember these men are gentlemen, just try to cool down and not be so obvious until you learn them a bit, ok?"

I winked my eye in hopes that she caught on. She winked her eye back at me, but I do not think she truly listened. Angel always wants to do things Angel's way. But at that moment—with eyes wide open—I saw Angel was empty too.

I looked at Heath to see his eyes fixed on Samantha, as if he couldn't believe what he saw. Oh, Oh, I thought. I walked over to Daniel and leaned into his ear. "Angel is into Heath, but it looks like Heath may be into Samantha."

"Oh—he is," he said swiftly.

"Ok, that was quick."

"Heath has a thing for redheads—always has."

"Red-haired woman…right…well, ok…."

I looked about as we shared thoughts, and there was Heath making his way over to Samantha. He didn't waste any time. Then I saw Angel making her way over to Samantha and Heath. "Well…ok… let's get started." Daniel and I looked at each other with enlarged eyes. We started with the rehearsal.

Almost three hours in, because we were fifty-five minutes over the scheduled time, we were about to leave. Thankfully, everybody there was full of smiles and anticipation—and gracious with the time spill over. As Purple and Sheila were heading out, Sheila grabbed me by the hand. "Opal, I can't wait. It's going to be so beautiful."

"Aww…" I stated, as I hugged Sheila.

"I can't wait either," Purple added. Then I hugged Purple. As I hugged Purple, Samantha and Heath caught my eye again from across the room.

"Ladies, did you check out Heath and Samantha?" They turned directly around.

"Don't make it obvious we are talking about them," I said swiftly.

"Chile, they wouldn't know anyhow, they were in each other's faces for at least two hours of the almost three hours we were here—yeah we saw it—you have to be blind not to see all of that."

"All in each other's faces…." Sheila added.

"Angel tried to interrupt," I said.

"Oh, honey, she tried…she tried…" Purple added.

"But that man is into our Samantha," Sheila replied.

"And Samantha is into him—can you believe that? Did you ever see Samantha smitten before?" I asked.

"I didn't think it was possible," said Sheila. Purple and I chuckled.

We then gazed around the room and found young Angel way in the corner with a glass of wine, nursing a saddened look as if a cloud of rain was following her.

"I think we should comfort our young sister. Sheila, won't you go over?" Purple suggested.

"Why me?" Sheila blinked.

"Because of your tender spirit. It's perfect for this moment," Purple said, matter of fact.

But I knew right then…

It had to be me.

I saw Angel's inner cry. Tanya's issue had me open.

CHAPTER 10

$\mathcal{M}$y tenth lingerie piece came out of a big, pink-bowed box.

"Daniel is going to have some fun," Samantha bellowed. We all laughed.

"Ms. O, I don't see why you won't let me get some strippers," Angel said, her eyes full of mischief.

"Angel—stop it. We are Christian women. Absolutely not!" I said. "We have good food, wine, games, and gifts—and most of all... we have each other. Anything else would be redundant."

"True. Plus, I wouldn't want no man's funky behind all up in my face anyway," Sheila added.

We all chuckled.

"Now that I had received all these gifts from you ladies—I have gifts for you," I said.

"No..." Purple and Angel groaned.

"I don't think so," Samantha interjected.

"Opal, it's your day," Sheila reminded me.

"No, it's not. It's really not. It's a day—and I choose to share it with you ladies. And it's a day you choose to share with me. For that, I'm very thankful."

"Amen," Purple chimed.

"You ladies are my friends and my sisters. Without your loving guidance, advice, counsel, and ear—I don't think I would be marrying the love God destined for my life."

Soft, charming "awws" floated into the room.

"Since the other ladies are gone, and my main ladies are here to spend the night with me—I can bring it out." The ladies started glancing at each other in confusion.

"Bring what out?" Angel said, beating the others to it.

"Yeah, what out?" Samantha echoed.

"Yeah…" Sheila followed.

I remained quiet, then rose from my chair and walked to the closet. I opened the door and pulled out a big purple velvet bag, like a modern-day Santa Claus. Returning to my seat, I slung the bag off my shoulder and began to pull out gifts, handing them out one by one.

Their faces lit up—and my heart beamed in response.

I reached down into the velvet again and again, pulling out surprise after surprise… until I reached my final gift.

The Wedding Day. Deep, resounding laughter caught our ears. We realized it was coming from outside. So, the ladies and I looked out the window and saw my Daniel and his groomsmen posing for the photographer. They were being silly, striking goofy poses. Of course, they took some classic gentleman shots too.

They were dressed to the nines in their white suits, threaded with gold—a detail woven delicately through their bowties and vests. It was interesting watching them from that window. Their personalities spilled out freely, unfiltered and alive. Daniel and the other groomsmen kept putting Professor Watts in the center of every creative shot. The ladies and I just loved it.

As they laughed and posed, a black Mercedes slowly pulled up and parked across the street.

I recognized that car from the other day.

"What is she doing here?" I said under my breath.

The ladies responded in unison.

"Who?"

"Tanya," I answered.

"Are you serious?" said Purple, her tone sharpened.

"I've been wondering what she looked like," Sheila said, leaning deeper into the window for a better view.

"How did she even find out where the wedding was?" Samantha spouted.

"Oh, I'm going down there—she done lost her mind!" Angel snapped. "Now she's trying to come and meddle on the day of the wedding?"

Angel started moving toward the stairs.

"Angel, no," I said, reaching out and grabbing her arm gently. "She's okay. She's no threat—she's fine."

All the ladies looked at each other in silence.

"Okay now, Ms. Cleverson," Purple said, "you slayed that dragon."

"In Him," I replied.

All the ladies responded in concert, "Amen."

We continued watching from the window as Tanya crossed the street. She wore only a plain white t-shirt and jeans, her face still marked up with visible bruises. And yet... she was still so beautiful.

I pray someone will make her happy one day, I thought, *and that she'll be able to make someone else happy too.*

The guys swarmed around Daniel like a web, sharing language we could only imagine. Tanya moved closer and closer to him with a small box in her hand, wrapped in a deep purple satin bow. All the men curiously eyed the box as she held it out to Daniel. His face sat still as he opened it.

"I wonder what they're saying," said Angel.

"Looks like she's giving him a wedding gift," Samantha observed.

"We can see that," Angel responded, "but what are they *saying*?"

We couldn't see what was inside, but we saw Daniel's expression shift—he was surprised. He then pulled out a card and started to read it. Oddly, seeing him that close to Tanya didn't bother me at all. It was amazing—there was no sting, no jealousy. I actually... sympathized with her.

After Daniel finished reading the card, he opened his arms to hug her. Tanya leaned into the embrace. Her shoulders began to move up and down slightly.

"Is she crying?" asked Sheila.

"I believe she is..." Purple added softly.

Tanya then let her arms fall to her sides in a defeated motion. She turned around and walked briskly back to her car, tears streaming down her face.

"That's sad," Angel whispered.

"It is…" I agreed.

I felt a pain for her—not because I wanted Daniel to be with her, but because I understood her story. I knew what Demitri did to her. I knew her desire for something she couldn't have. Of course I was grateful Daniel was mine, but I also felt Tanya's emptiness, her war, her loneliness. I felt it… through the window, watching her hurry back to her car.

And in that moment, I realized—things often aren't what they seem. I had gone from disliking that woman, very highly… to mourning for her in a way I didn't expect.

An hour later, there was a knock at the door. Samantha, being closest, called out, "Who is it?"

"Jordan," came the voice from the other side.

Samantha cracked the door open. "Yes?"

She and Jordan exchanged a few whispered words I couldn't quite make out. Then she closed the door and returned holding a familiar box—the same purple-wrapped box Tanya had been carrying earlier.

Samantha walked over to me and handed me that box, it certainly was the box that I wondered about—we wondered about.

"What was that about?" Sheila asked Samantha.

"Daniel wanted me to give this to Opal," Samantha said, walking over to me.

It felt like slow motion. Curiosity wrapped around all of us as the ladies and I gathered around *the* box—the same box we'd seen through the window, the one Tanya had given to Daniel.

I opened it.

Inside was a golden key, laying on top of a card.

I picked up the key and studied it. It wasn't a modern key— nothing like a house or car key—but it was definitely a key to something. Symbolic, perhaps. I carefully opened the card, and inside it read:

"Daniel,

I am so sorry things ended the way they did between us, but at the same time, I am grateful. Knowing you allowed me to know love. It helped me see myself—and those around me. And meeting your soon-to-be wife showed me I was never really the woman for you—but she is. I'm thankful to have met her, even briefly.

I will always love you. But I know I must let you go in my mind and in my heart—in a certain way, at least. As you always told me, in marriage the two become one. In this box you'll see one key. It was meant for you—but if you are to be 'one' soon, then it is for you both.

This key is symbolic. It means you were the key—the key to me finding true love and breaking free from the chains of Demitri.

I can almost hear you telling me now that God was the key, not you. But as you said, He works through people. And I saw God work through you. I also saw Him in Opal. Thank you—for being a sweet witness."

Drops of water landed on the card.
But I didn't feel anything falling from *my* eyes.
I looked up.
It was Sheila—hovering over me, tears flowing freely.
My nosy sisters…
I looked around at the other ladies and they had understanding and fullness on their faces. I immediately bowed my head and began to pray for Tanya. And the ladies joined me.
I looked in the mirror—and I felt beautiful.

Yes, I had on *the* dress—the one that called me by my full name. It knew me, and I knew it the moment I saw it. It was classy and elegant. It complimented my silhouette, and with the long train trailing behind me, I could already imagine someone whispering: "Queen Opal has entered the building."

My makeup was soft and neutral—barely there.

My curly tresses were pinned up, leaving my self-made baby hairs to frame the masterpiece. My curls were adorned with a side pearl and crystal head comb—big, classy, and fabulous. I wore chandelier earrings and a beautiful crystal bangle that adorned my wrist with quiet radiance.

I looked in the mirror again. And I realized…

It wasn't so much the image before me that made me feel beautiful.

I felt beautiful because I felt—loved.

Loved truly. From my Daniel to my sisters.

I turned towards the ladies and marveled for a brief moment at them as they talked amongst themselves. It seemed their nerves were as bad as mine. They looked like they felt the moment with me. As if they felt the last walk I was about to take as a single woman. I was undoubtedly about to become something more within a matter of minutes, converge Cleverson with Pacini. We all had continuously flooded eyes that we had to keep swiping with a tissue. Sheila was crying so much, she had to keep reapplying her makeup.

The drama.

Those church doors were in front of me, and I was behind them with a subtle anxiety and a sobering realization, the realization, that at that moment, I was starting a new season in my life.

This was it.

The wedding party and I were about to take our positions to walk down that anxiety-ridden aisle. But Purple walked in front of me.

"Words from a matron of honor," she began. "Remember—*we women are the ribs of our husbands*. We carry an intuition and an insight that he needs—and you must never forget that."

She paused, her eyes locked on mine.

"Opal, do you remember that day you were so heartbroken over you and Daniel, you could barely walk up my cobblestone steps? And I had my husband help you—even though he was wobbling himself?"

"Yes," I said softly. "I was wondering about that..."

"What you didn't know," she continued, "was that Pastor Chris was having a hard time just before you arrived. He was feeling low—like his surgeries had slowed him down and made him...useless."

She exhaled deeply before going on. "So I had to speak life back into him—remind him who he was. And sometimes, to do that, you've got to find small or big situations where he can *find himself within himself again.*"

I nodded, listening with my whole heart.

"I know Daniel is what you'd call a *man's man*—so is my Chris. But even the strongest of men will have their moments. And you, Opal—you're going to have to speak life into him. There will be times you'll need to open his eyes, even though he's as brilliant as he is."

She touched my arm gently.

"He needs you, just as much as you need him. And your calling... is to pull out the king in him—even when he's acting a fool, and to pull out that king when he seems to be discouraged. And most of all, your function is to be love and be loved."

I nodded again, eyes softening. "Amen."

"That's good," Professor Watts chimed in with a warm smile. "She's right."

We all giggled.

"Thank you, Purple," I said, wrapping my arms around her before she walked to her place.

Then, Professor Watts gently offered his arm, and I looped mine through his.

Suddenly, the music began. The doors opened.

Purple walked down the aisle first. She wanted to walk alone—and honestly, she was a vision all by herself. Regal. Strong. Wise. Then came Samantha and Heath, followed by Jordan and Sheila, Mike and Angel, and Bobby with my cousin Dee Dee. And then—

My adorable godson, as cute as he wanted to be, came darting around the corner and *ran* down the aisle. You could tell he was still running, even though he'd been told to walk slowly. The room broke out into laughter. Thank goodness that ring bearer didn't actually have the ring.

Next, my Goddaughters walked out to the isle, almost dancing down in all innocent joy, dropping purple flowers. The church walls echoed with awes and flashes of light lit up the room.

Then...

The doors closed again.

Professor Watts and I stepped behind those grand church doors. He looked at me with a final, proud glance.

"My Daniel found the right one," he said, his smile stretching wide.

I smiled back.

The music shifted.

The doors opened again, slowly—pulling out every last drop of anticipation.

I was in awe.

The church looked breathtaking. April had added some last-minute touches, and everyone looked so joyful. The way the sunlight poured through the stained-glass windows made the entire room feel more elegant, more romantic... almost divine.

And then my eyes, which were enthusiastically dancing around the church, stood still, because they found him. Daniel.

The density of my love for him hit my heart it seemed all at once, it hit my heart so much that I felt a subtle hint of hurt.

He looked so handsome—even more handsome than ever before—and I didn't know how that was possible. I walked down the aisle slowly with Professor Watts. I saw all the faces lining the pews, many with tears, all with wide smiles and grins as I passed each one. Then I looked back at Daniel. He was turning pinker with every step I took toward him. Tears began to fall down his face. He was trying to hold it together, but he couldn't. His response made me respond the same.

It felt like I was walking in slow motion. Then Daniel began walking toward me. He stepped down the marble steps and gently reached for my hand, guiding me up the stoop. Together, we stepped forward until we stood before Pastor Chris.

"Stop it—you're making me cry," I whispered.

"You look so beautiful," he said, as his chest went in a little. It was like he was being pressed and sweet aromatic emotions poured from his heart.

He bent in to kiss me, but Pastor Chris quickly stepped in.

"Hey, hey—not yet."

Daniel froze and everyone burst out laughing—even Daniel.

"You'll get your chance. Just calm down, son."

Laughter echoed through the sanctuary like music.

Then Pastor Chris began to speak—words of covenant and responsibility, then a blessing over our marriage. There was prayer, then singing, and even a bit of dancing. And then... it was time. Time to say the words that sealed the covenant. Time to become one.

Pastor Chris raised his preacher's voice with joyful authority and turned to Daniel.

"Do you, Daniel, take Opal to be your lawfully wedded wife? Will you love her, comfort her, honor her, protect her, and provide for her—to have and to hold from this day forward, for better or worse, for richer or poorer, and, forsaking all others, keep yourself only unto her, so long as you both shall live?"

"I do," Daniel replied, eyes locked on mine.

Then Pastor Chris turned to me.

"Opal, do you take Daniel to be your lawfully wedded husband? Will you love him, and honor him, and comfort him—to have and to hold from this day forward, for better or worse, for richer or poorer, and, forsaking all others, keep yourself only unto him, so long as you both shall live?"

"I do."

As I said it, I was pulled into a *marvelous revelation*—time suspended for just a moment.

God was revealing parts of Himself through Daniel to me this whole time. Daniel could've left me for a more intelligent, prettier woman, in all of his handsome and intellectual grandeur, but he loved me, just for me. And that... that is how God loves.

In all His splendor, He desires a relationship with us. The real part of us.

I thought of that scripture in Psalms: *"What is man, that You are mindful of him?"*

Tanya had tried to steal that kind of love—tried to earn it with beauty and works. But it fell flat. Demitri tried to *manipulate* love, to control and possess the glory that only God holds. And he fell flat too.

But the seeking—the authentic search to know, created true love—relationship did this. The seeking of God created a relationship with Him.

It is something that can't be manipulated or modified—but just sought. Now, as I stated, God worked through Daniel. Daniel is a fallen person like the rest of the world, but I saw how God was communicating through him. He was defining the art of love—through the seeking, through relationship.

Daniel had to seek me. And I, him. He had to walk with me and I, him, so that he could pull out that wounded, insecure girl inside of me—so she could be healed. And only then could I truly see others in a way that would help heal them.

I realized in that moment just how much my Father—Yahweh, Adonai, my Creator—had gone through to help me understand this truth.

I cried gentle cries as I looked into Daniel's eyes again, then lifted my gaze into space.

"To God be the glory!" I shouted.

Daniel lifted his eyes upward as well.

"To God be the glory!"

He looked back at me with a stare of amazement. Then, with a hushed and reverent tone, his deep voice poured out:

"O my love, you are as beautiful as Tir'zah, Lovely as Jerusalem,

Awesome as an army with banners! Turn your eyes away from me,
For they have overcome me.

I joined.

"*My beloved is white and ruddy, Chief among ten thousand. His head is like the finest gold; His locks are wavy, and black as a raven. His eyes are like doves by the rivers of waters, washed with milk, and fitly set. His cheeks are like a bed of spices, banks of scented herbs. His lips are lilies, dripping liquid myrrh. His hands are rods of gold set with beryl. His body is carved ivory inlaid with sapphires. His legs are pillars of marble Set on bases of fine gold. His countenance is like Lebanon, excellent as the cedars. His mouth is most sweet, yes, he is altogether lovely. This is my beloved, and this is my friend, O daughters of Jerusalem!*"

We exchanged rings.

Then Pastor Chris stirred up his preacher's voice with joyful power:

"By the power invested in me, I now declare you husband and wife! Now—you may kiss the bride!"

A loud roar erupted through the church walls, echoing celebration.

Daniel pulled back my veil—and we kissed.

And as we kissed, it was as though all our emotions exploded in fireworks. We giggled, teared up, and embraced each other with every press of our lips—passionately, reverently, wholly.

Coming up for air, Daniel whispered, "I love you."

"I love you," I replied—my voice carrying a subtle depth that even surprised me.

Daniel shivered slightly, as if a cool wind had run up his back.

"You okay?" I said, gently rubbing his arm.

"I can't wait."

"Me too," I smiled.

We both chuckled.

I grazed my fingers across his glorious black wavy beard, and he looked at me with those amazing greenish-chestnut eyes with its tints of amber.

"I have sought you and found you, my bride," he said,

"A heart after my heart—my Shulamite Woman."

SHULAMITE WOMAN

*O*pal laid her head on Daniel's chest, listening to the rhythm of his heartbeat. The sunrise hit their faces through the window. They interlocked their fingers while their faces held a warm fulfillment.

A faint buzz interrupted the divine silence.

Her phone lit up on the nightstand. Unknown caller.

She hesitated. *It was so early. Who would be calling at this time—It must be important—who would call this early if it wasn't?* Her thoughts rushed. She picked up.

"Hello?"

A pause.

Then that creepy voice.

"Hello… Princess."

Her stomach knotted. She abruptly sat up in the bed and turned towards Daniel. Reading her face, he abruptly sat up as well.

To be continued…?

ABOUT THE AUTHOR

*J*aneen Chambers is a gifted Creative Writing and Performance Arts creator, originally from Pittsburgh, Pennsylvania. With a background in Mass Media Communications and Sociology, she shares powerful stories that empower, challenge, encourage, and inspire. Her artistic reach spans videography, photography, dance, music, and, most notably, creative writing. Over the years, Janeen has used each of these gifts for one central purpose: **to tell a really good story.**

ELF&E

Shedding light through creativity

Printed in Dunstable, United Kingdom

71539003R00077